What Readers Are Saying About
DIARE OF A TEENAGE GIRL SERIES...

Sold Out

"Melody Carlson's latest installment in her Diary of a Teenage Girl series gives readers an engaging speaker in Chloe."
—*Romantic Times* Book Club Magazine

My Name Is Chloe

"Readers will delight in this edgier, more intense, electric guitar-playing lead character."—*Publishers Weekly*

"*My Name Is Chloe* should be read by every teenager and makes a great crossover book or ministry tool."—*Christian Retailing*

On My Own

"i love all the books cause they relate to my life in some way or another."—ABBIE

Who I Am

"It's so refreshing to read about the life of a Christian girl for once. I can't get enough!"— JAMEY LYNNE

"This is such an amazing, inspirational book and i have gotten so much out of it."—AMALIE

"This was so cool!! It actually helped me w/my real life!! I even prayed some of the prayers that she wrote down!"—HEATHER

"Wonderful! Another perfect book to go along with the first two."—DANI

"I really enjoyed it. When I read it, it made me realize my commitment to God was fading. Since them I have become rejuvenated and more committed."—ERICA

It's My Life

"This book inspired me to persevere through all my hardships and struggles, but it also brought me to the reality that even through my flaws, God can make Himself known in a powerful, life-changing way."—MEGHAN

"This book is unbelievable... It's so absolutely real to any teenage girl who is going through the tribulations of how to follow God. I've just recently found my path to God, and I can relate to Caitlin in many ways—it's a powerful thing."—EMILY

"I loved it!! It was so inspirational and even convicted me to have a stronger relationship with Christ. Thanks Melody, this is the series I've been waiting for!!!"—SARAH

Becoming Me

"As I read this book, I laughed, cried, and smiled right along with Caitlin. It inspired me to keep my own journal. It changed my life forever. Thank you."—RACHEL

"I love all of the books! I could read them over and over!!!"—ASHLEY

"I couldn't put it down. When I was finished, I couldn't wait to get the second one!"—BETHANY

Diary of a Teenage Girl

Chloe Book Nº. 3

road trip

a novel

MELODY CARLSON

Multnomah® Publishers
Sisters, Oregon

ROAD TRIP
published by Multnomah Publishers, Inc.
and in association with the literary agency of Sara A. Fortenberry

© 2003 by Melody Carlson
International Standard Book Number: 1-59052-142-0

Cover design by David Carlson Design
Cover image by Steve Gardner/His Image PixelWorks
Based on original artwork by Reza Estakhrian/Getty Images

Scripture quotations are from:
The Holy Bible, New International Version
© 1973, 1984 by International Bible Society,
used by permission of Zondervan Publishing House
The Holy Bible, King James Version

Multnomah is a trademark of Multnomah Publishers, Inc.,
and is registered in the U.S. Patent and Trademark Office.
The colophon is a trademark of Multnomah Publishers, Inc.

Printed in the United States of America

For information:
MULTNOMAH PUBLISHERS, INC.
POST OFFICE BOX 1720
SISTERS, OREGON 97759

04 05 06 07 08 09 10—10 9 8 7 6 5 4 3 2 1

One

Monday, August 30

It's been almost three weeks on the road now, and I hate to admit it, but some of the glitz has worn a bit thin lately, or maybe it's just getting tarnished. At least for this girl anyway. On the other hand, Allie is still flying higher than a Pop-Tart. Between Allie, Laura, and me, Al's probably the best candidate for a life of fame and fortune. Not that we've seen too much of that since we've only played the state and county fair circuit so far, hanging out with the cows and quilts and raspberry preserves. We've seen more of the Midwest than I ever imagined existed and logged more miles than I can track. I suggested we get one of those maps with stickers of the states on it, but Allie said that would be lame. I'm not so sure.

We've also hit a few "mega churches" along the way. Last night we performed in a Colorado Springs church with about five thousand people in attendance. Just your average Sunday night service. Talk about overwhelming. I can't imagine ever fitting in at a church that size. Although

I'm sure it works for some people, and the pastor seemed like a pretty cool dude. Just the same, it really makes me appreciate my little church back home where I know everybody by name.

Anyway, I think we've done about ten performances so far. Even so, it's safe to say that "Redemption" hasn't exactly become a household word yet—at least not as far as the name of our band goes. Hopefully the word "redemption" is still common in most households.

And backing up here, I don't mean to criticize Allie about her seamless adaptation to our new "celebrity" status. Although sometimes I expect she'd like to do an interview with Robin Leach, telling him about how fantastic it is for a drummer to suddenly be living the lifestyle of the "rich and famous." Ha.

But to be perfectly honest, I think sometimes I almost envy her. Like the way Allie can walk into a room holding her head at this cocky little angle as she coolly scopes out the situation from behind her wire-rimmed purple shades. (I think this is becoming her signature.) And I'm rather impressed with how this sixteen-year-old girl can put out that rock star persona and actually get away with it. Whereas I feel completely stupid and conspicuous whenever I act like that. And believe me, I've tried it a couple of times.

"Just chill," Allie told me yesterday when I

was trying to sneak away from an impromptu signing that was making me feel claustrophobic. "This is no biggie."

I rolled my eyes at her, then forced a smile to our gathering of "groupies," who appeared to be in middle school.

"She's just shy," Allie told the girls who were patiently waiting for her signature. "She'll grow out of it someday."

At least this made them laugh. But I still felt dumb. Maybe I'm just incredibly insecure or socially inept. I'm not even sure what exactly it is that impairs me in this particular area. But the sad fact is: I feel unbearably self-conscious sometimes. Now that probably makes absolutely no sense when you consider how I like my appearance to be slightly shocking, or at least that's what some people say. To me, I look perfectly normal. I mean, sure, I've got my piercings, my eggplant-colored short hair, and what some people consider a weird wardrobe, although it suits me. But those are not the things that make me self-conscious. It's something else entirely. I'm not even sure what—well, other than basic don't-look-at-me-too-close insecurity. Fortunately, I don't feel like that when I'm onstage playing my guitar.

Thank God, I am perfectly comfortable up in the lights when we're performing. It's as if all my fears just melt away. I'm sure I'm more comfortable than Allie up there, since she still suffers an occasional bout of stage fright. Although she hasn't barfed on my guitar recently.

Still, it bugs me that I do come slightly unglued when we're just hanging and people start pointing or staring at us as if we've just been beamed down from a UFO. And I don't particularly like it when they ask for our autographs. But Allie thinks it's totally cool. She literally thrives on it. I just don't get it. For the life of me, I don't know how a person can prepare herself for this kind of intense attention.

I mean, talk about weird—having perfect strangers walk up and ask you to sign your name on their programs or T-shirts or, on the rare occasion when they've actually purchased our album, on CD covers. I've even been asked to sign Bibles, but I refused. Then if that's not bad enough, one time this guy walked up to me and pulled up his shirt and invited me to sign his chest! Okay, I've seen Allie sign people's hands and arms, but I'm thinking we have to start drawing the line somewhere.

I guess I never considered this side of the business before. I always thought having a band and doing concerts would be about the music. But now I can see it's a whole lot more, and I have a feeling I don't know the half of it yet. As a result, I've noticed that whenever I start to feel uneasy or intimidated by a particular situation, I start to slip back into my "tough chick" exterior. I don't like that I'm doing that, but it just feels safer somehow. Hopefully no one has noticed. Allie and Laura haven't mentioned anything yet.

Speaking of Laura, she seems to be handling everything fairly well. Or at least on the outside. Sometimes it's hard to tell exactly how she feels underneath because she's so good at keeping up appearances. If she ever gave up music, she could take up acting. Fortunately, her self-control and smooth restraint make her pretty cool and dependable onstage. And then when we're done performing, she's really warm and friendly with the fans on the sidelines. She comes across as generally well-balanced with her all-around steady-as-she-goes kind of style. I suppose I envy her a little bit too. Naturally she has no idea.

It's kind of funny to consider how different the three of us are. What a trio! And sometimes it just totally amazes me that we ever got together in the first place. How did that happen? Definitely a God-thing.

We recently came up with a little routine that we do before a concert. It's our way to determine who gets to share her testimony. It only took a couple of concerts before we all agreed that it's better not to know when your turn to speak was coming. That way you don't get quite so nervous beforehand.

So, about five minutes before we hit the stage, the three of us huddle together on the sidelines and do the old rock-paper-scissors routine. Naturally, the "winner" gets to speak to the crowd. Not that we think of it as a win-lose type of thing; mostly we just hope that God is in control of the choosing that day.

After the "speaker" is selected, we finish off with a quick prayer. We always pray for the audience, that God will reach out and touch their hearts through our music. And so far, so good. Or so it seems. It's hard to know for sure, but the general reaction of our audiences has been quite positive.

As a result of our little elimination game, I've come to think of the three of us in those same terms—rock, paper, and scissors. I see Laura as the rock since she can be so immovable sometimes, but she's also dependable and solid. Allie is the paper because she can be kind of flighty, but at the same time she's flexible, fun, and active. I guess that makes me the scissors, which doesn't seem like such a great thing really. But maybe it's because I'm the songwriter and I have to be on the cutting edge—ha. Naturally, I haven't told Allie and Laura about my little metaphor.

Somehow I don't think they'd fully appreciate it.

Now, just in case it sounds as if I'm complaining, I'm not. I am thoroughly enjoying our tour. And the scenery's not bad either. Like right now we're driving through some of the most incredible country I've ever seen—amazing mountains and trees and beautiful sunsets. It's been awesome! I feel totally blessed by God, and every single day I'm thankful for all He's done and is doing with our band.

ROCK, PAPER, SCISSORS
three together
fitting in
yet so different
set apart
made by One
who knows all things
knows our weaknesses
and our strengths
hold us close
within Your hand
use us for Your glory
amen

Two

Friday, September 3

(ENTERING OREGON)

It's weird to think that all of our friends are thinking about going back to school next week. Meanwhile, Laura, Allie, and I are totally reveling in the knowledge that we're free from that sort of drudgery. What a trip! Oh, sure, we've got our textbooks and will be connecting on-line for assignments, but it sounds like we'll only need to spend a few hours a day actually doing schoolwork. And man, does that feel good.

Sure, I miss my friends, and even my family sometimes. I probably miss Cesar the most, but we stay in touch through e-mail. Life's so full and busy that it's hard to get too homesick.

Although Laura admitted to me that she's been struggling with it. "I don't want to sound like a whiner," she told me as the two of us were flopped out on the bed in back of the RV. "But I really miss my mom."

"Why don't you call her?"

"She'd be at work right now."

"Oh."

"Don't you miss your mom, Chloe?"

I shrugged. "I guess so. But you know that my mom and I aren't that close. Not like you and your mom."

"Yeah. I suppose."

I could tell by the tone of her voice that she was feeling sort of down. "Are you okay?" I rolled over onto my stomach and studied Laura's face. Her dark eyes were looking down at the brown and green comforter on the bed as her fingers traced the floral pattern. Now Laura has the most beautiful hands. Not only the bronze color of her skin, but her fingers are long and slender and tapered, the way you'd expect a musician's to be. (Although mine are rather short and stumpy.) "What is it, Laura?"

"I just get scared sometimes, Chloe. I don't want the others to know. I really don't want to let any of you guys down, but I get worried that I won't be able to keep up."

"Keep up?"

"The pace, you know? You and Allie have so much energy. Sheesh, Allie's practically bouncing off the walls half the time. I'm just not used to this kind of life."

"But I think you're doing fine."

I could see tears building in Laura's eyes now. "Thanks."

"You gonna be okay?"

She shrugged. "I guess."

"You're probably just tired," I reassured her. "You want me to leave you alone so you can take a nap?"

She swiped what I suspect was a tear with the back of her fist, but she didn't say anything.

"It's going to be okay, Laura. You just need to go easy on yourself. We're all still getting used to the pace. But really, I think you're doing great. I mean, just the other day I was thinking about how well you handle everything."

She nodded, pressing her lips together. "Yeah, I guess I make it look that way."

"But you don't feel like that inside?"

"I feel like Jell-O on the inside."

I smiled. "What flavor? Grape? Cherry?"

She frowned. "Very funny."

"Sorry. Is there anything I can do to help you?"

Laura shook her head. "You're probably right. I think I'm just tired. Maybe if I could get a good night's sleep, things would look better."

"You aren't sleeping well?"

"Not really. I thought it would get better with time, but it's like I'm so wired when it's time to go to bed. And then I hear noises and stuff. I know it sounds lame, but I've always had a hard time sleeping away from home."

I didn't know what to tell her. But I could see that she was really feeling worried. "Have you talked to your mom about it? Or Elise or Willy?"

"No, but I guess maybe I should."

"Yeah." I reached over and tweaked one of her beaded braids. "We need you to be at your best, Laura. For your sake as much as the band's. I'll leave you alone so you can take a nap now. Okay?"

She leaned back and closed her eyes. "Sure."

So now I'm sitting at the dining table, writing in my diary. Rosy said that we just entered Oregon, but it doesn't look much different than Idaho. It's attractive with rolling hills and farmland, but it looks pretty sparsely populated in this area. She said that we're going to follow the Oregon Trail along the Columbia River, but at the moment, we're whizzing by what I'm guessing is a grainfield. Maybe wheat, although it could be anything. It's a warm golden color, but the grain's already been harvested, and what's left looks like a bad buzz haircut.

Elise is sitting on the couch across from me, reading one of Allie's fashion magazines as she runs her fingers through little Davie's sweaty hair. He's taking a nap at the moment.

It's been fun getting to know Elise better these past few weeks. When I first met her last year, I thought she was a little high-strung and uptight. But now I realize that had a lot to do with her circumstances—having gone through a lousy divorce and having a handicapped child.

Plus there was Allie with her hyper thing.

I guess Elise's life hasn't been exactly easy. But the coolest thing is how she gave her heart to God right after our last Nashville trip. It started with a conversation she'd been having with Willy on the flight home. And of course, we three girls had really been praying for her too. But after we got home, Allie convinced Elise to come to church. And Pastor Tony actually gave an altar call that day. I've only seen him do that a few times.

Well, Elise stood and went right up. Afterward, we were all crying and hugging, and I could tell that something in Elise had changed. Even her face looked different. It's as if something in her just relaxed. Of course, she's had plenty of trials since then. And chaperoning us girls isn't a job that just anyone would appreciate. Still, I can see that she's really trying her best. And every day she reads the new Bible that Allie bought her.

Davie's been a handful today. He even spilled a carton of chocolate milk down Rosy's back while she was driving on the interstate this morning. She was <u>not</u> happy. As much as we all love him, Davie can get a little wild at times. But like so many kids with Down's syndrome, he has such a sweet and loving nature that it's hard to get too upset. Anyway, things are pretty calm and quiet right now. Hopefully, Laura is getting some much needed rest.

Allie's up front quietly chatting with Rosy. I think Al's trying to make up for her little brother's earlier mishap. We all think Rosy's a kick, and we love hearing her stories. Allie thinks she looks like Queen Latifah, but fortunately she doesn't use the same kind of language. We take turns visiting with Rosy as she navigates this big rig down the highway.

We're supposed to make Salem by dinnertime tonight. And we're performing at the state fair the following evening. So we'll have two nights in one town. Unless we're driving a long distance—pulling an all-nighter—we usually stop at a hotel every night. There we have the option of either sleeping in the RV or getting rooms. Most of the time I opt for the RV, since all my stuff is already in here and I hate having to drag it all out.

Elise, Allie, and Davie usually get a hotel room together, while Laura and I stake out the RV with Rosy as our chaperone. And if Laura and I had any ideas about sneaking out or doing anything stupid—which we really don't—Rosy, who's almost six feet tall and pretty hefty, could easily stop us.

Sometimes Allie hangs out in the RV with us at night. But she really doesn't like having to share the little bathroom. But I think the RV is kind of homey and comfortable and lots better than a boring old hotel room.

Although I'll admit it can get pretty cramped when Rosy is driving an all-nighter and all five of us are forced to sleep in here. Still, it's doable. On those nights, two of us girls share the big bed—usually Laura and me. Then there are two pull-down bunks (for Allie and Davie) and a couch that makes into a bed, which Elise sleeps on. I suppose it's not ideal, but it works. And I usually sleep like a log.

I feel bad for Laura today. I had no idea she was so tired and worried about things. I'll need to remind myself to pray for her more.

GOD'S LULLABY
blow Your breath upon her
as You hold her in Your hand
wrap her in Your serenity
peace we can't understand
comfort her with Your presence
as You gently close her eyes
rock her in Your arms, Lord,
as You sing sweet lullabies
amen

Three

Monday, September 6

(LABOR DAY, DRIVING THROUGH NORTHERN CALIFORNIA)

We did three concerts in two days—our record so far—and we're all feeling pretty wiped out. On Saturday we did the Oregon state fair. Then on Sunday we played for a pretty big church in Eugene, Oregon. Then we zipped down to a smaller town called Ashland, where we performed an evening concert for a medium-sized church. Our reward for all this hard work is that we get to camp in the mountains tonight.

"You call that a reward?" complained Allie after Willy told us the news over breakfast at Denny's this morning.

He grinned. "Sounds like a reward to me."

"What exactly do you mean by 'camping'?" asked Laura with one brow raised. "Do we have to actually sleep outside?"

Willy chuckled. "Only if you want to."

"No thanks," said Allie.

"Count me out," agreed Laura. "I have enough trouble sleeping in the RV. I don't need to be freakin' about things like bears or snakes."

"Suit yourselves." Willy shook his head with

23

an expression that suggested he thought we were a bunch of sissies. I wanted to say that I was perfectly willing to sleep outside but didn't want to make Allie and Laura look bad. So I kept my mouth shut. But the truth is, I thought it'd be cool to sleep out under the stars and the moon. And as we drove through this gorgeous forested area (Lassen National Park), I thought maybe I would. I just didn't make a big deal about it. Especially since Laura seemed a little stressed out.

I asked her last night if she'd told her mom about her sleeping problem.

"Yeah, she said that she'd call Dr. Stewart. He's a friend of the family. She thinks he'll recommend something." Laura shook her head. "In the meantime, she told me to drink a glass of warm milk."

I made a face. "Yuck."

She nodded. "Just what I was thinking. I mean, I can barely stand to drink cold milk. Like I'm really going to drink it warm."

We pulled into a campground that looked like something out of an old Disney movie. I spotted lodge-type buildings and small cabins located here and there as we followed Willy's RV and snaked our way around a gorgeous blue lake. Willy had the right idea—this place was totally beautiful. I couldn't wait to get outside and check it out. And Davie was so excited to escape the bus that he was literally bouncing off the walls. Poor Elise looked as though she'd about had it. But Rosy quickly parked the bus, and like clowns in a circus car we all poured out of the RV, breathing in the clean mountain air and whooping like grade-schoolers on a field trip.

(Later the same night, I am writing by flashlight)

Our camping excursion has been totally cool. Even Laura and Allie are liking it. As soon as we got outside, we walked over to the camp store and bought some treats, then rented a rowboat to take out on the lake. We rowed out to the middle to a floating dock where a bunch of other kids were hanging and swimming and stuff. They invited us to join them. So we tied up our boat and got out. It was getting pretty hot, so we decided to jump in the water and cool off. We splashed around for a while until we got tired and climbed out.

So there we were, just relaxing and contentedly sunning our tired selves on the dock, and Allie let it "slip out" to these kids that "we were in a band." Amazing how she managed to do this. She can bring up our "celebrity" right out of the complete blue. Honestly, people could be talking about lobster traps in Maine, and somehow Allie would be able to connect that with the fact that we're in a band!

Laura looked somewhat irritated as she shook the water from her braids, and I was downright embarrassed, but Allie went right on telling these guys about all the concerts we've done and how we have our own CD and everything! Sheesh, I actually wanted to smack her. But I didn't. Finally, Laura and I hinted that we should get back, and Allie actually invited these kids over to our campsite. I'm thinking, "Okay, now you've gone too far." But I didn't say anything. I just climbed into the boat and pretended like I wasn't totally irritated with her.

"You want to swim back to camp, Allie?" I asked as I began to paddle away from the dock.

"Hey, what're ya doing?" she yelled.

So trying to be a loving Christian, I forced myself to row back to the dock and wait until she climbed in. But as we paddled away, Laura lectured Allie about her big mouth.

But I have to say it really didn't turn out so bad. Not long after dinner, about six of these kids dropped by our campsite, I'm sure out of curiosity.

By then Willy had made a little campfire, and I was playing my acoustic guitar, just tweaking around. Elise had brought out the ingredients for s'mores, and we were all pretty much sugared out. Anyway, we welcomed these guys and offered them some s'mores. Then we sat and visited for a while. They said they lived in a nearby town and were camping on their own, enjoying their last bit of summer before school started in a couple days. They actually reminded me of some of my friends at school, the kind of kids who pretty much do as they please and whose parents don't seem to much care.

As usual, Laura made it perfectly clear from the start that we were Christians. And that was okay with me, but I don't think she had to be quite so up-front about it. Sometimes I think it's fun to let it slip out naturally. But as it turned out, one of the guys—a sixteen-year-old named Brian—had a lot of questions about our faith.

"Yeah, my mom claims to be a Christian too," he admitted as he poked the fire with a long marshmallow-toasting stick, "but she just kicked me out of the house."

"Why?" I asked.

"She thought I was doing drugs and stuff."

"Were you?" asked Allie in a gentle voice.

He shrugged. "I was trying to quit."

"Trying?" repeated Laura with one of her skeptical Laura-looks. He didn't answer and she continued. "You know, a person could spend his whole life 'trying' not to do something, but it's only when he decides he's not going to do it that he succeeds."

Brian looked up at her and finally nodded. "You might be right."

"It can be pretty hard to quit something like that on your own," I told him. "But it can make a huge difference if you ask God to help you."

"You really think that God—if there is a God—really listens?" Brian studied us carefully as he waited for an answer.

"Yeah," chimed in a girl named Stacie with a tattoo of a black rose wrapped around her wrist. Her hair was cut short and dyed maraschino cherry red. I'd already complimented her on it earlier today. I'd try that color myself except that I'd have to bleach my hair first to get it to be that vivid. At the present I'm settling for this deep purple black shade. "What makes you think God even cares?" she asked with a defiant tilt to her chin.

"I used to think he didn't," I told her.

"Me too," added Allie.

Then I proceeded to tell these kids about how I questioned God and life and just about everything until I got so depressed and desperate that I cried out to God to help me. I told them about meeting God in the graveyard—how I stumbled upon Clay Berringer's gravesite and the powerful words on his headstone. "Jesus said, 'I am the way and the truth and the life,'" I quoted to them. "He said, 'No one comes to the Father except through me.'" I then explained how reassuring this was to me personally—just knowing that Jesus is the One who paid the price for me to have a relationship with God.

It wasn't so different from what I say at concerts when it's my turn to share my testimony. But somehow, sitting by the campfire with these kids listening right next to me, it felt more real than ever. And I suppose I spoke with an urgency that I don't normally feel. My face flushed with intensity, or maybe it was the heat of the campfire, but I felt almost embarrassed when I finished. Not from speaking the truth, but from being a little pushy.

"Sorry," I said quickly. "I didn't mean to sound all preachy or anything."

"It's okay," said Brian. "A lot of what you said makes sense. I guess I've felt the same way sometimes."

"Me too," echoed another girl who'd been quiet until then.

"It's kind of like this song..." said Allie.

I tossed her a warning look. No way did I want this evening to turn into a mini concert.

"Aw, come on, Chloe," she urged me. "Can't we sing 'Stubborn Love' to them?"

Laura nudged me with her elbow. "Yeah, aren't we supposed to sing around the campfire, Chloe?"

Willy snickered as he pulled a sleepy little Davie onto his lap.

"Okay." I sighed and picked up my guitar then started strumming. "You guys might be sorry you stopped by. Who knows, we might end up singing "Kum Ba Yah" or something equally lame before the night is over."

So the three of us sang "Stubborn Love," and when we finished, the kids actually began to clap.

"That was so cool," said Stacie.

"Yeah," agreed another girl. "You guys are really good."

"Sing another one," urged Brian.

I noticed some movement in the shadows beyond the campfire and looked up to see several bystanders lurking about. "Hey, you guys might as well join us," I called out. And so we sang a few more songs, and believe it or not, we even ended the evening by singing "Kum Ba Yah."

Pretty funny. Actually, it was pretty cool. We talked a little more, and I think some of the things we shared were sinking in. I plan to pray for the new friends we made today—that God will chase them down with His stubborn love.

CAMPFIRE PRAYERS
twilight and firelight
faces warm and flushed
open hearts and open minds
and in Your spirit rushed

starlight and moonlight
here beneath the deep
i place myself in Your hands
and peacefully i sleep
amen

Four

Tuesday, September 7

(DRIVING INTO NEVADA)

It's funny to imagine our friends back in school today. Can't say that I envy them, stuck in those suffocating classrooms while summer continues to lurk outside their windows. It still feels as though we're on vacation. Okay, a working vacation.

Anyway, we're heading to Reno right now. Not to gamble but to perform. I suppose that's a bit of a gamble though. I mean, it seems as if the day could come when all we get are lemons—like a crowd that really hates us. I'm not even sure what I'd do if that actually happened. But I've dreamed it before. Actually, it was more of a nightmare.

We're standing onstage, and I can't remember how to play my guitar, and the whole audience is booing and throwing shoes and stuff at us. It's so humiliating. When I wake up, I try to remind myself that we're performing for God, not man, and if people quit liking us at least God still will. Even so, that nightmare always leaves me feeling unsettled and insecure. As a result, I'm sure I push Allie and Laura even harder when we rehearse the next day. But it's not nearly as hard as I push myself.

We drove through Donner Pass this morning—the place where the settlers got stranded in the snow and ate each other. Well, I'm sure that's oversimplifying the whole thing, but it does leave you with an eerie feeling. I don't care how hungry I was, I don't think I could ever resort to eating a human. It was hard to imagine that such a tragedy could've occurred in a place that looked so pretty and green and peaceful. But we saw photos of how it looks when the snows come, and it's a totally different scene.

Laura was feeling somewhat relieved today, since we were able to pick up her prescription to help her sleep. I sure hope it works. She's been getting pretty cranky lately. Allie told me it's really due to the fact that Ryan Hall hasn't e-mailed her since August.

"Laura's afraid he's going to forget all about her in college," Allie whispered as we lounged in the back bedroom, supposedly working on lyrics.

"Maybe it would be for the best," I said. "Then she could focus more on our music."

"Don't tell her that."

"I guess I didn't realize she had it that bad for him." I frowned as I tweaked a word in the second stanza.

"Yeah, sometimes it's hard to tell with Laura.

She's pretty good at keeping her feelings hidden, you know?"

"I suppose." But it surprised me a little that she'd shared this tidbit with Allie and not me. Now as I write this, I'm trying not to feel jealous because I'm glad that Laura told someone. But at the same time, it makes me feel a little on the outside of things. But I suppose she thinks I wouldn't understand since I'm the one who's always saying we need to put our music first, especially now that we're officially on tour. (I mean, first over guys—not God!)

Hopefully, her sleeping pills will help her get some rest and she'll start acting like her old self again. While I personally don't like the idea of using medications for anything (I hardly ever take an aspirin, but that's just me), in Laura's case I can understand. She's been so stressed and tired that I'm sure it's not good for her to continue like that. It's not good for any of us. Maybe her little blue pills will make the difference.

Allie is still her lively old happy fun-loving self. And as usual, this is rubbing Laura all wrong. Lately, she's been getting irritated at Allie for almost everything. Like talking too much or bouncing around the RV like a Superball—just the normal Allie stuff. But I feel sorry for Allie too. I know she feels cooped up and gets tired of being picked on for her "vivacious" personality.

As a result, she often chooses to ride in Willy's little RV. But I know he appreciates the company. In some ways I think Willy is becoming a real father figure for Allie, and that's cool. I can tell that Elise really appreciates his influence.

Anyway, this calms things down in here a lot, and I can usually manage to get some songwriting done while Allie's gone. Of course, there's still Davie to contend with, but Elise does a pretty good job of keeping him occupied. It's funny because Elise, although energetic, is a fairly calm and controlled sort of person, but her kids, as sweet as they both are, are still a handful at times. In fact, I overheard Elise talking to Allie yesterday while we were packing things up after our camping trip.

"Maybe you should consider going back on your Ritalin," she said in a quiet voice. I'm sure she didn't realize that I was just around the corner shaking pine needles from my sleeping bag.

"Why?" Allie asked in this slightly whiny voice that she always reserves especially for her mom.

"I think your hyperactivity gets on Laura's nerves," continued Elise. "I'm sure you don't realize it, honey, but you can be pretty irritating sometimes."

"But I hate how those pills make me feel, Mom.

It's like they completely sap my energy, not to mention my creative juices. You know how they turn me into Zombie Girl."

"But they do calm you down."

Allie sighed loudly. "Okay, fine! But how about if I try to calm myself down without the pills first? Maybe I could tape my mouth shut and put a pillow over my head. Would _that_ make you happy?"

"Oh, Allie."

"Then maybe you guys would quit picking on me."

"I'm not trying to pick on you. I'm just trying to—"

"I know, Mom. You're just trying to help."

"Well, the pills are in the medicine cabinet if you change your mind."

Poor Allie. I shook my head as I finished rolling up the sleeping bag. But I don't blame her a bit. I sure wouldn't want to have to take pills to calm me down either. It's weird to think that Laura needs pills to help her sleep and Allie needs pills to calm her down. Sheesh!

But I must agree with Allie on this. I think she's perfectly fine without her Ritalin. In fact, life would be sadly boring if Allie suddenly started acting all quiet and calm—or grumpy like Laura. I guess I need to let Allie know that I like her just the way she is—live wire or not. Allie is just Allie, and that's okay by me.

WHO WE ARE
who are we
and what's our game?
all are different
none the same
each unique
and different face
each one goes
a different pace
God has made us
to go far
in our own way
who we are
cm

Thursday, September 9

(DRIVING THROUGH NO MAN'S LAND)

It's pretty bleak and barren out here in western
Nevada. I think they used to test nuclear bombs
somewhere around here, back in the dark ages, or
maybe it was the fifties. And as opposed as I am to
weapons of any kind, particularly nuclear, I could
almost understand how those scientists might've
assumed that there was nothing they could hurt
out here in the middle of nowhere. It is so desolate.

And yet the more I look out upon it, the more
I'm starting to appreciate it—the rock forma-
tions, cactuses, and warm desert colors. I guess

it's starting to grow on me. The scenery is sort of hauntingly lonely, and it makes me wonder how I would feel if I were out here all by myself. Just God and me, hanging out in the desert together.

Naturally, these are the kinds of thoughts I keep to myself. I don't think either Allie or Laura would understand completely. I know they think I'm a little extreme sometimes. But maybe Willy would since he's had some interesting experiences during his somewhat unconventional life. And perhaps Rosy would too, being a lady truck driver and all. I imagine her as something of a free spirit.

Well, Laura's sleeping pill seemed to work just fine last night. In fact, she was so knocked out this morning that Rosy took off driving down the highway even before Laura woke up. We decided not to disturb her since she's been so exhausted lately. Elise said it'll probably take her a few days to catch up on her z's.

It didn't help matters that we were out rather late last night. I think we're all fairly worn out. Our concert was at a big church in Reno, and we'd agreed to meet with the kids in the youth group and answer questions afterward. I think we all lost track of the time because it was nearly mid-night when the youth pastor told us we'd have to call it quits. But it was fun seeing the excitement of this youth group.

They're launching a "Reach Out to Reno" campaign for the fall. Their goal is to touch every
high school kid with the gospel by Christmas.
It's a pretty huge undertaking, but they seem to
be up for it. We promised to pray for them as well
as have Willy look into the possibility of return-
ing here for another concert at the end of the
year. I'm not sure how that will go since it seems
our schedule is already pretty much booked up.
At least that's what Willy said.

"You girls are almost finished with your
break-in tour," he told us at lunchtime today.

I pointed to a zit that has just emerged on my
forehead. "You mean our breakout tour."

"Gross," said Laura. "I'm trying to eat here."

Allie poked me in the arm. "Told you not to
scarf down those chili fries last night."

"Anyway..." I could tell Willy was trying to get
us back on track. "A couple more gigs and we're
heading to Los Angeles."

I watched Allie's eyes grow big at the sound of
that. We all know that LA is supposed to be the
big turning point in our career, the place where
we go from county fair fledglings to legitimate
concert musicians.

"So when do we get to meet them, Willy?" Allie
drummed her fingers on the table. "When's the big
day?"

Willy attempted to look confused. "Who?"

"You know who." Allie tossed her straw at him. "Iron Cross. The Baxter Boys. Jeremy and Isaiah, for Pete's sake."

"Oh, them." Willy nodded as he stroked his chin. "Well, you girls are scheduled to open for them on September 24."

"Wow, that's only a couple of weeks off," said Allie. "You really think we're ready for the big time, Willy?"

"The powers that be at Omega Records seem to think so. And they've scheduled about five days before the concert for you girls to practice up. Eric Green will be flying out in the middle of the week to determine whether or not you're ready for this."

"What if we're not?" Laura still looked slightly groggy, but at least she wasn't too cranky.

"We will be," I assured them. "We'll start practicing our vocals more on the road. And we'll spend more time warming up before our concerts. I suppose we've gotten a little lazy."

"Lazy?" echoed Laura. "I feel like I've never worked harder in my life."

"Okay, maybe 'lazy' isn't the right word. But I think we can use the next couple of weeks to really improve. I know I don't want to embarrass Iron Cross with a mediocre performance."

Allie nodded. "I'm game."

Laura nodded too, but her enthusiasm level seemed lower than usual. Hopefully she'll get better with a few more good nights of sleep.

So we spent the rest of the afternoon working on vocals and memorizing lyrics and daydreaming about the night when we'll actually open for Iron Cross. It still feels too good to be true.

FLYING HIGH
head in the clouds
feet on the ground
sometimes i feel
like i'm spinning around
my heart is so happy
i'm flying so high
i wanna stay grounded
and whiz through the sky
hold on to me, Jesus,
help me to stand
and follow Your lead
as i take Your hand
amen

Five

Monday, September 13

(LEAVING LAS VEGAS)

Now, I don't like to sound like a country bumpkin, but Las Vegas is one freaky place. It's as if everything there either sparkles or blinks or shines. Talk about flashy. And although it's not my cup of tea, I must admit that it was somewhat fascinating.

We did two church concerts over the weekend. Yes, there are churches in Las Vegas, as well as plenty of Christians too. Okay, the churches are a whole lot different than what I'm used to back home, and I have to remind myself not to judge them. Or any of the people we come across, for that matter. After all, I should know as well as anyone how it feels to be judged by appearances. And I must give these churches some credit for allowing us to perform, since we must look pretty strange to them.

Anyway, our music seemed well received and, if I do say so myself, I think we're improving. Willy said so too. But I'm still concerned about something. Or rather someone. It's Laura. She just doesn't seem to be herself lately. I'm not sure if the sleeping pills are dragging her down or whether she's moping about Ryan or if she's just totally wiped out by our tour.

I talked to Willy about it this morning.

"You gotta understand that it takes some people longer to adjust to all these changes of life on the road," he told me as I rode the first leg of our trip with him, supposedly to get some help on the arrangement for a new song.

"But how long?" I asked with all the patience of a jackrabbit.

"Hard to say." He turned up the air-conditioning. "It's different for everyone. And Laura's a very serious and sensitive girl. Besides that, I think she's used to her routines."

"But we have routines."

He laughed. "They may seem like routines to people like you and me, Chloe. We're both pretty free spirited and like flying by the seat of our pants. But it's harder on Laura."

"I've really been praying for her, Willy."

"I know. We all are." He nodded. "Don't worry; I'm sure she'll get better with time."

"How much time?" I'm wondering. We've been on the road for over a month. I'd think she'd have adjusted by now. I don't know what we'd do if Laura was unable to tour and perform. It's scary to even think about. With only three members in a band, it can sound pretty lame when one is missing or even just slacking off. Without Laura, I feel fairly certain that Omega would cancel our contract, not to mention our tour. At the same time, I'm telling myself not to freak about this, but to do like the Bible says and just pray. Still, it's a pretty big concern.

I had an e-mail from Cesar today. Of course, I didn't tell Laura this. No need to make her feel worse about Ryan's lack of communication. Actually, Cesar has been faithful to e-mail me almost daily, but we don't always get to stop somewhere to check it.

Willy said he's going to figure out a way for us to go on-line while we're on the road. Naturally, he says this is so we can keep up with our schoolwork. But we think it'll be nice to keep up with our friends and family.

Anyway, Cesar was talking about the beginning of school and how boring it was there without us (that was kind of good to hear). He also mentioned how Tiffany Knight was bragging to everyone how she and I are such good friends now, and I must admit that she e-mails me a lot. But I think it's pretty funny considering how she used to try to beat me up on a fairly regular basis, back before I became "famous." Oh, well.

I also had an e-mail from Caitlin. Her sophomore year of college has started, and she's rooming with Liz Banks again. Good old Caitlin, hanging in there with a girl who couldn't be any more opposite to her Pollyanna personality. But she said that Liz has been changing a lot, and Caitlin thinks they have the potential to be almost as good of friends as she's been with Beanie Jacobs. Now, that would be something.

Better not let Beanie in on this little news flash. I can't believe how much she helped us to get our traveling wardrobes together for this trip. Naturally, we paid her. She said we didn't need to, but we insisted. We really wish we could bring her with us to help us get ready before every concert, although it is pretty cool that she got accepted into design school this year. Maybe when she graduates she can come and work for us.

Anyway, hearing how everyone back home is doing, I get the feeling that life goes on...whether you're part of it or not. And it's kind of weird to feel removed like that. Although life has been going on for us too—at a pretty fast pace. Did I really think my old world would simply stand still because I'm not in it? How childish is that? But I guess I feel as though we're living in a whole different universe right now. Nothing is the same. And all my old friends and family seem so far away, so out there and removed. It feels pretty weird and slightly scary.

Yet at the same time I'm really okay with it. I guess it's just the price you pay to follow your dreams. <u>Things change.</u> Still, I tell myself that I will make a better effort to stay in touch with everyone, go the extra mile if I need to. Because, really, I don't want to lose them. I've heard so many stories about rock stars and actors and how they get all rich and famous and eventually lose touch with their old friends. I never want to be like that.

DON'T WANNA CHANGE

don't wanna change

or rearrange

or be estranged

or get deranged

don't wanna lose

or hafta choose

or be cut loose

or just refuse

don't wanna take

or be a fake

on the make

what's at stake?

don't wanna try

and wonder why

friendships die

then sadly cry

don't wanna blame

it all on fame

we're all the same

just kinda lame
don't wanna stay
the same old way
every day
so i pray
i wanna be
God in me
help me see
i'm set free
cm

Six

Saturday, September 18

(DOING DISNEYLAND)

Okay, Las Vegas was sorta strange, but LA is a real trip. It's like a world unto itself. How can I even describe it? Yellow murky skies hang over-head, although I've heard people say it's not always like this. It's very hot and dry, and palm trees seem to grow everywhere. Lots of cars and bumper-to-bumper traffic that rushes along until it comes to a complete halt. You'd think the freeways would be piled high with wrecks, though I've yet to see one.

But it's the people who get my attention. Everyone down here just seems to have this atti-tude going on. Okay, not everyone. But a lot of folks go around acting like they're really impor-tant or have important business to attend to with their fancy cars and suits and cell phones. It's hard to explain, but I do find it rather intrigu-ing. And once again, I'm trying not to judge. But it's okay to observe. I like observing.

Speaking of observations, I'm still worried about Laura. I think those sleeping pills are grogging her out. It's like she's losing her edge or something. It's even starting to show in her music. Not that she's making bad mistakes or anything obvious, but she's just not herself. It's like she's turning into this zombie. Willy even mentioned something to her yesterday afternoon.

"You feeling okay, Laura?" he asked as we packed up after our concert in Anaheim. We'd done another church thing, and while it had gone relatively well, it felt as if something was missing onstage. At least it did to me, but apparently Willy had noticed it too.

She just shrugged and zipped up her bass case. "I guess so."

"You getting enough sleep these days?" he asked.

"Yeah, I think—"

"Hey, are we still going to Disneyland today?" interrupted Allie.

"Not you," teased Willy. "I heard they don't let blond drummer girls in there anymore."

Allie punched him and they started teasing each other, and Laura's lack of energy was brushed under the rug again. But she did seem to perk up in Disneyland. We joked around and laughed a lot while we waited in long lines for rides—no celebrity treatment there. Although

Allie did make a couple of lame attempts for special treatment, but no one was falling for it.

We stayed until the fireworks show, but by then poor little Davie was really dragging. I can't say that Disneyland was the greatest thing I've ever experienced, but it was fun in a kiddish way. The whole place sorta reminded me of this gigantic movie set—totally unreal. But then that's Disneyland for you.

LAYERS OF REALITY
what is real?
what is not?
do you know
what you've got?
will it stay?
will it last?
will it fade?
shrinking fast
will it keep
you safe from harm?
is it real
or just a charm?
trust the One
you cannot see
His real truth
will set you free
cm

Wednesday, September 22

(HANGIN' AT THE HOTEL)

We've done nothing but practice-practice-practice the last three days. Oh, yeah, that and schoolwork. There seems to be no getting out of schoolwork. Elise is our taskmaster where the books are concerned. And she's relentless.

I think Willy is worried about us. Mostly Laura. It's almost like she's not really here. I'm not sure what's up with her, but she's scaring me. She did admit that she's sad about Ryan. She still gets tired a lot, but at least she's been sleeping soundly every night.

The real problem is that Eric Green will be here tomorrow. He's coming to make sure that we're ready to open the concert for Iron Cross. Willy said that after Eric listens to us, we get to have dinner with the guys from the band. So naturally I'm feeling pretty nervous. But not as nervous as Allie. She's wound so tight that I'm expecting her to totally lose it by the time she lays eyes on those "beautiful Baxter boys" as she likes to call them. I'm sure she's already in love with Jeremy.

And then we have our laid-back Laura. It's as if she's walking around in this foggy cloud, just plodding along. I hope she can get it into gear by the time Eric stops by to listen to us tomorrow.

This afternoon, while we were taking a short break by the hotel pool, I asked her if she thought she could pull this thing off.

"What do you mean?" she looked at me as if she had no idea what I was talking about.

"I mean, you." I tried to choose my words carefully since there's no point in getting her upset. "You've been in such a funk lately."

Laura looked down at the towel in her lap and shook her head. "I don't know what's wrong with me, Chloe."

"None of us do."

"Willy asked me if I needed to see a doctor today."

I turned and peered at her. "Are you sick?" She looked healthy to me.

"I don't feel sick. Just sort of down and tired. I do miss Ryan, but I'm trying to move on. And I'm still a little homesick, I guess, but I've been feeling better about that lately. It's been relaxing staying in one place for a while."

"Yeah, this is a nice hotel. But I'm actually starting to miss the old bus."

She sighed. "You're so well suited for this kind of thing, Chloe."

"And you're not?"

"I don't know."

"Are you sorry you signed on to do the tour?" Now this was the question that's been nagging me for weeks, but I've been afraid to ask.

"No. I love being part of the band. But lately I feel so guilty because it seems like I'm dragging you guys down."

"Have you been praying about this, Laura?"

"Yeah. And it helps, but it's just so..." She shrugged. "Oh, I don't know."

I didn't know what to say then. It was almost time for us to be getting back for our final practice session. "Well, can't you just try harder, Laura?"

She nodded. "Yeah."

And I think she did manage to crank it up a notch during our next practice. When we finished I felt slightly encouraged. And Allie looked relieved.

"Good job, girls," Willy said as he started unplugging our equipment. It's really been great being able to use the same room to practice in all week. No setup or teardown.

I put my guitar in the case. "You think we'll make the grade?"

"I'm sure Eric will be pleased," he said with a somewhat reassuring smile. I wasn't entirely convinced, but I'm trying to think positively.

I'm hoping that we're getting back into our groove now. Hopefully Eric won't be sorry that Omega signed us. We'll see tomorrow.

NO REGRET
do your best
give your all
be the most
heed your call
live your life
use your gift
then you'll feel
your spirit lift
don't hold back
from all you get
go all out
no regret
cm

Seven

Thursday, September 23
(HIGHS AND LOWS)

Eric took Willy out for a little consultation after he listened to us play. I could tell something was wrong.

"Did I blow it?" asked Laura after the guys left.

I shrugged, avoiding her eyes. "I don't know."

"Well, we sure weren't very good," said Allie. I could tell by her flushed cheeks that she was really frustrated.

"You mean I wasn't very good," Laura said with what looked like tears in her eyes.

"Don't beat yourself up." I was trying to sound soothing, but I'm afraid I sounded mad.

Laura unplugged her bass. "I should just quit."

"Yeah, that'd be just great," Allie said as she hit the cymbal hard. "You quit and we're finished. Our illustrious music career will be shorter than the one-hit wonders."

Laura sat on a folding metal chair and held her head in her hands. "I'm so sorry, you guys."

She was crying now. I went over and stood next

to her, putting my hand on her shoulder as I tossed Allie a look that said, 'Get over here this minute.'

"I think we need to pray," I said.

"Yeah, come to think of it, we've been getting a little lax about that," said Allie as she came over to join us.

And right there in the practice room Allie and I both asked God to help us. We prayed that He would touch Laura and give her whatever she needed to finish this thing.

"We're here to bring You glory, God," I prayed with heartfelt urgency. "We want to be Your instruments. Please, help us to continue using our gifts. And use us to get Your message out."

"Amen," said Allie.

"Amen." Laura looked up and wiped her eyes. "I think I'm going to do better now."

"Really?"

She nodded with a look of determination. Just then Eric and Willy returned.

"Eric has some concerns," said Willy.

I took in a quick breath and focused my eyes on Eric. I knew what was coming. He was about to announce that our contract had been dissolved. Redemption was no more.

"I realize you girls have been working really hard," began Eric. "And it's difficult getting up to speed when you're just starting out. It's natural to struggle with all the demands of your schedule and performances. And all that stress can even affect your music, but—"

"It's all my fault!" Laura exclaimed. "I'm so sorry. I haven't been—"

"I'm not here to point the finger at anyone," continued Eric. "I just want you to know that I understand how it goes."

"But it's not Chloe and Allie." Laura folded her arms across her chest. "I'm the one dragging the band down."

Eric nodded. "That might be true. But the fact is, it takes all three of you being at your best to make it in this profession."

"I know that," said Laura. "We were just praying about it, and I feel certain that everything is going to change."

Eric didn't seem convinced. "Look, it's not like we're going to cancel your contract or anything. I just think maybe you're not ready to open for—"

"We are ready!" demanded Laura. "I feel like something has really clicked in for me. Won't you at least give us a chance?"

"It's not that I don't want you to have a chance, Laura. I don't want to risk introducing you to the public when you're not, well, when you're not at your best."

"But I can do this." Laura was getting that old stubborn look in her eyes again, and I began to feel a little bit hopeful. "Honest, I know that I can do this. Everything will be different tomorrow night. I promise."

Eric looked torn as he held his hands up in the air. "I don't know what to do."

"Can't you let us try?" I asked. "I know Laura well enough to believe that if she says she can do something, then she can."

"Are you willing to risk Redemption's reputation with a bad opening?"

I glanced at Laura to see a spark in her eyes then said, "I don't think it will be a risk."

"How about you, Allie?" asked Eric. "You've been awfully quiet."

She nodded. "I'm with Chloe. I don't think it'll be a risk either."

He carefully studied all three of us. "You're absolutely certain about this?"

We all nodded in unison.

"How about you, Willy? Think they can pull this off?"

Willy grinned. "I know they can."

Eric blew out a long sigh. "Okay, it's settled. I just hope it's not a mistake."

"It isn't," Laura assured him. "Things are going to be different from now on."

I hope and pray that she's right.

"So, are you girls ready to meet the guys?" Eric asked as he glanced at his watch.

"You mean Iron Cross?" said Laura with wide eyes.

He nodded.

"Don't we get to go clean up and change our clothes first?" Allie frowned as she looked down at her white T-shirt with its mustard stain from lunch still slopped down the front.

"Of course. Why don't you meet us downstairs at six-thirty."

So we rushed back to our rooms and spent the next hour trying to look presentable. Between the three of us we must've tried on fourteen different Beanie Jacobs outfits. Fortunately, we were so obsessed with our appearances that we didn't have time to discuss what had almost happened today. I ended up wearing a black velvet skirt with my purple Doc Martens and a retro top with beads and fringe. I think I looked pretty hot. Allie wore a short lace dress from the sixties that Beanie had found at a flea market; she paired this with her tall lace-up boots.

"Where's Laura?" asked Allie as she put on some pale pink lipstick.

"She had to go down to the RV to get a pair of shoes." I held up a tube of dark purple lipstick. "What d'ya think of this color?"

"Ooh, I think it'll look hot on you."

Finally Laura came back. She had on a sleeveless lime green dress and matching sandals.

"What do you think?" she said as she turned around for our inspection.

Allie pressed her lips together then nodded. "Very cool."

Elise and Davie decided to forego the dinner. "Davie spent too much time at the pool today," she explained. "He's got a sunburn and really needs to go to bed."

"Are you sure, Mom?" asked Allie. Although I could tell by the look in her eyes that she was relieved. I'm sure she thought she'd appear much more grown-up without her mother along.

Elise nodded. "I know you'll be in good hands with Willy."

As soon as the elevator door closed, Allie burst into an uncontrollable fit of giggles.

"Get ahold of yourself, girl," I told her.

"You're going to embarrass us," warned Laura.

"I can't help it," Allie sputtered. "I'm so excited that I think I'm going to literally burst—just splatter all over this elevator."

To our relief, Allie finally managed to control herself just as we stepped into the lobby.

"Okay," she said, holding her head at that cocky little angle as she slipped on her sunglasses and put on her sophisticated smile.

"You're really going to wear those shades to meet them?"

She nodded. "It's who I am, Chloe."

Now I started giggling. Laura jabbed me with her elbow as we walked across the lobby to where Willy and Eric and four very good-looking guys were waiting. We were formally introduced to Jeremy and Isaiah Baxter. Jeremy is the older brother at twenty-one and Isaiah is eighteen. The other two guys, Brett James and Michael White, are nineteen and twenty, respectively. They've been playing together for about five years.

I was so nervous that it was hard to eat dinner, and I'm afraid I didn't speak very much. I hope the guys don't think I'm a complete idiot. To my surprise and relief, Allie and Laura both did a good job of keeping the conversation going.

"Chloe's the songwriter," Allie said with what seemed like honest pride. I smiled at her, thankful that she was helping me not to look like a total fool.

"Yeah," said Laura. "She's got a notebook full of songs we haven't even recorded yet."

"Jeremy writes most of our stuff," said Michael.

Jeremy put his hand on his brother's shoulder. "Hey, Isaiah's been turning out some pretty great lyrics lately."

"But it's hard to compete with big bro." Isaiah poked his brother in the arm.

"Redemption has a great sound," said Jeremy.

"We've been playing your CD a lot."

I felt like I was about to faint just then. Not that I've ever been a fainter before, but hearing Jeremy Baxter from Iron Cross say that they've been playing our CD was just way too much.

Fortunately for me, we called it an early night. I'm really not sure how much more I could've taken. I mean, these guys are totally cool. I know they're just normal human beings like the rest of us, but I must admit to feeling totally starstruck tonight.

Even as I sit here by the window and write down these words, I feel like pinching myself. Is this real or is it all a dream? I feel higher than a kite right now, and I'm worried that I'll never be able to go to sleep tonight. Laura took one of her "magic pills" and is already sacked out and actually snoring. As usual, she and I are sharing a room. Is Allie as wired as I feel? I'd go over and knock on her door, but I'd probably disturb Elise and Davie. So I simply sit here and bask in the mere wonder of it all.

And I refuse to think about the possibility that it could all blow up in our faces tomorrow. Instead, I pray that Laura keeps her word, that God performs some kind of amazing miracle, and that Redemption plays better than ever before and Iron Cross is totally jazzed to have us for their warm-up band. Hey, it could happen.

HIGH HOPES
my heart is so light
i feel i can fly
like a midnight star
across the sky
i'll dance with the moon
and float on a cloud
i'll play a new tune
and praise God aloud
cm

Eight

Friday, September 24

(THE BIG NIGHT)

All day long I have been nothing but a great big pile of jumping, jittering, jangling nerves. I honestly felt as though I could've taken up smoking today—now, how lame is that? But it's like I needed something to do to distract myself, something to calm me down. Naturally, I prayed a lot, but there were times when my prayers sounded slightly crazy, even to me. It's a good thing that God can see straight into our hearts when we speak to Him. I'm pretty sure He can sort the whole thing out.

We started out the day with a morning practice, which was absolutely and unequivocally rotten. Laura was barely awake and pretty grouchy, and Allie kept getting on her case until Laura started crying and saying she was hopeless and useless and why didn't we just kick her out of the band. We finally ended up quitting early and going our own separate ways. Willy didn't say a single word. I think he was feeling pretty freaked. I know I was.

Then later this afternoon, it seemed as if

something just snapped in Laura. I mean, a good kind of snapping. It's like she suddenly came back to her old self. Only way more so! For the first time in weeks, she was animated and happy and really excited about the concert. I think it was God's answer to our desperate prayers—a real walking and talking miracle.

And when we stepped onto that stage tonight, I felt totally stoked and energized, like: "Yeah, we can do this!" And man, did we ever! Redemption rocked! I think it was our best concert of all times. I know I was totally blown away by the sound. Laura and Allie were really hot, and we were all just jiving together like we used to, only better. It was so incredibly cool. And the crowd really seemed to like us too. We even got encored. Later on when we were signing CDs, Jeremy told us that Iron Cross was getting worried, thinking it wouldn't be long before they would be opening for us. Ha. Now that'd be the day.

Anyway, I was so relieved that we didn't blow it, I would've settled for an okay performance. But this was something way better. Laura was so happy afterward that she broke down and cried again. Only these tears, I'm certain, were pure relief.

"You did it!" Eric said when he caught up with us backstage between the shows. "Praise God! You girls really did it!"

We were so jazzed that we wanted to go out to celebrate. Eric hired a limo to take us, along with Rosy, Willie, Elise, and Davie, to an all-night ice cream shop, where we ordered the works and totally porked out. I think this has been one of the best nights of my entire life. Really, can it get any better?

Tomorrow we head out, actually touring with Iron Cross. Thanks be to God, we passed our initiation test—now let the fun begin!

Still being somewhat of a realist, I fully understand that anything could go wrong, even now. That little episode with Laura was enough to knock us out of the concert circuit for good. But I'm not going to worry about it tonight. I'm going to trust God to continue taking care of us—I know He can get us where we need to go. And Laura has assured everyone that she's going to be fine from here on out. She said that it was just a temporary funk but that she has everything under control now. And I believe her since it seems like she's totally back to her old self—even better!

PRAISE GOD
just when i wanted to pull my hair out
You came through
like You promised You would
just when i thought the morning wouldn't come

You showed up
and brought the sun with You
just when it seemed like it was all over
You started it up again
with Your freshness and life
i praise You, my God
i thank You for miracles
and i trust You with whatever comes next
amen

Thursday, September 30

(SOMEWHERE BETWEEN SAN DIEGO AND TUCSON)
We did our second concert with Iron Cross last
night in San Diego, and it went just as well as the
first one. Maybe even better. The best part of the
whole evening was when we got to hang with these
guys after the crowd was gone. I think what surprises me most is how these guys come across as
just ordinary guys, like you might know from
school or whatever. Well, in an extraordinary
way, I guess, because they all seem so spiritually
mature to me. I suppose they should be since
they've been Christians a lot longer than I have.
(Jeremiah and Isaiah grew up in a strong
Christian home.) Also they've had a pretty successful band for nearly five years, and I'm sure
that helped them to grow up. But even so, they're
not full of themselves and don't have that "rock

star" mentality. They're cool.

"So what do you think of all this?" asked Isaiah as we sat around backstage just eating chips and drinking sodas.

Now, as I'm recording all this in my diary, which could be made into a movie someday (okay, I may be slightly delusional), I wonder how I would describe these handsome guys. Well, first off, Isaiah is really good-looking, with dark brown eyes and short dark hair with long sideburns. But there's something else about him that's hard to describe. Maybe it's like charisma or personality. But when they're all onstage he almost seems to sparkle. Of course, I wouldn't say that to him. I mean, what guy wants to think he sparkles?

Anyway, he plays a really mean keyboard and almost makes me wish we had someone else in our band to play keyboard for us, but I'm getting distracted. Now Isaiah and his brother Jeremy look quite a bit alike, but Jeremy's hair is long and he wears it pulled back in a tail. Also he sports a pretty cool goatee, which makes him look older (and he is). He's quieter than Isaiah and lots more serious. Jeremy plays guitar.

"All this what?" asked Laura with a twinkle in her eye in response to Isaiah's question.

Isaiah held out his hands and grinned. "All this rock star glamour and prestige."

We all paused to look around the messy dressing room with its beat-up couches and old vinyl chairs, and then we just laughed.

"Pretty impressive," I said as I reached for a handful of sour cream chips.

"Some performers would have a total hissy fit about a place like this," said Brett James. He's the drummer and has this really great smile and blond-tipped hair.

"What do you mean?" asked Allie, and I hoped she wasn't getting any prima donna ideas. "What would they do?"

"Some performers get details about dressing rooms written right into their contracts," Brett continued. "Like they have to get nice furniture and fresh flowers and specific kinds of food and all kinds of stuff."

"You're kidding," I said. "Do they really get it?"

"If they've got big enough names."

"Well—" I rolled my eyes—"we won't have to worry about that."

"Oh, I don't know," said Allie, getting that dreamy diva look in her eyes.

I firmly shook my head. "No way. Besides, even if we ever did get to be a big name like, say, Iron Cross, I think it would be really lame to act that demanding."

Jeremy nodded. "That's how we feel too."

"Yeah," agreed Isaiah. "It's fun having folks cater to you, but we try to remember that we're here to serve."

"That's been a big part of our ministry," said Michael. He'd been pretty quiet most of the evening. He has extremely curly reddish hair that's cut short. He plays bass but, with his lanky arms and legs, looks as if he'd be more comfortable on a basketball court. That is, until, you seeing him getting down on his bass. Then he totally looks like a musician.

"The thing is," continued Jeremy. "Like Isaiah said, we really do believe that God gave us our gifts to serve others. And that helps keep everything else in perspective."

"Not that some people don't forget sometimes." Isaiah glanced over at Brett.

"Yeah, yeah." Brett shrugged. "I'm only human, you know. Sometimes it's fun to enjoy the stardom a little."

Allie nodded. "That's how I feel...sometimes anyway."

"I'm sure God doesn't mind if we enjoy our little perks." Isaiah held up a cheese curl with yellowed fingers. "Like this fine cuisine they provide for us."

We all laughed.

Then Jeremy made this sweet little speech about how they really thought we had talent and they wanted to do anything possible to help us.

"We really mean it," he finished up. "Whether it's music-related or your own spiritual walk, we're here for you."

The other guys nodded, then Michael looked at his watch. "Well, we're here for you for a few more minutes. Then we gotta split to catch our flight."

"You guys are flying to Phoenix?" asked Allie with wide eyes.

Jeremy shrugged a bit sheepishly. "We used to have to travel by bus too. But things change, you know?"

"Hey," I waved my hand, "we understand. You guys have paid your dues. It's only fair."

"And sometimes we go in our bus," said Jeremy.

"Yeah, especially with the way security is getting," Brett added. "You practically get strip-searched every time you try to board a plane."

Allie grinned. "Maybe they just think you guys are cute."

"Seriously?" said Laura. "They even make celebrities go through all that security?"

Isaiah laughed. "Yeah, that's one place where there are no respecters of persons."

"It's a good way to bring you back to earth," said Jeremy. "Just in case you're getting a big head." He jabbed Isaiah with his elbow.

"Anyway, we'll probably ride on our bus from Albuquerque to Santa Fe, right, Jeremy?"

"That's the plan."

"Cool." Allie had two stars shining in her eyes as she waved good-bye to Brett. It was all I could do not to burst out laughing. That girl has absolutely no sense of subtlety. I originally thought she had it bad for Isaiah, but as it turns out, she's smitten with Brett the drummer. Guess it takes one to know one. Still, I'm guessing these guys already have girlfriends. I know they have plenty of girl fans who would be perfectly willing to volunteer if they don't.

Now, as I sit here writing in the privacy of my diary as our bus rolls up the highway toward Phoenix, I will admit which guy (in Iron Cross) most intrigues me. I guess I shouldn't be too surprised by this since I've always considered him to be the best looking in a dark, serious way. Of course, all I had to go by was their album covers before. But anyway, it's Jeremy Baxter. Okay, Allie might not think he's such a hottee—at least not in her book—but I happen to think he is totally gorgeous. Although I will probably keep this to myself.

Because of course, I know he's way too old for me. Sheesh, he's even older than my brother Josh. But I can't help but think he's pretty cool. And mature. I really like the way he talks about his relationship with God. I guess I just really respect him. It's not as if I'm having a crush or anything. That would be childishly stupid. Besides, I'm still sort of involved with Cesar. Or at least I think I am.

To be honest, I'm beginning to think it's a little weird having this long-distance relationship with a guy who I probably don't know all that well. I realize, especially by his e-mails, that Cesar considers me his girlfriend. And I suppose I felt like that last summer. But I'm not so sure anymore. So much else is going on now. I guess it's not really important to figure this out tonight. But just the same, I'd feel awful to think I've been disloyal to him. Cesar is one of the coolest, most grounded guys I know. Which reminds me, I need to e-mail him tomorrow.

WISH-WASH
sometimes i don't even know
what's going on in me
i think everything's all clear
and then i just can't see
wish-wash, wish-wash
which way to turn?
wish-wash, wish-wash
will i ever learn?
i think i know my way
i'm gonna do it right
and then i'm all confused
my mind is outta sight

wish-wash, wish-wash
what is right to do?
wish-wash, wish-wash
God, how i need You
only You can lead me
whether east or west
i trust my way to You
the One who knows me best
cm

Nine

Sunday, October 3

(COOKING IN PHOENIX)

Man, is it hot down here. And crowded. I am seriously wondering what makes all these people want to live in a hot desert spot like this. It's not that the landscape isn't beautiful—in that stark desert sort of way. But according to what I've heard, most people seem to stay inside with their air conditioners cranked up all the time. I suppose the heat could take its toll. There will definitely be no sleeping on the bus down here. Too stuffy.

We've done three concerts with Iron Cross so far. I'm almost beginning to feel comfortable with the whole thing. And fortunately, Laura is hanging in there just fine. Oh, she still has her slumps and gets grumpy sometimes, but when it's time for a concert, she really comes to life. In fact, she's been great every night we've performed. So it seems we're over some sort of hump here.

And from now on our schedule will be a little less demanding than it was when we were doing the church and fair circuit, but the expectation level is much higher. We've got to be in tip-top

form every time we open for Iron Cross. Willy and
Elise keep reminding us to pace ourselves. I'm
sure they're worried that we could easily become
burnt-out before our tour is up.

Willy finally got our laptops hooked up to
some kind of wireless service so we can use the
Internet while we're on the road. So now we have
no excuse not to stay in touch with everyone—as
well as getting our homework done. Already I've
hinted to Cesar that this long-term relationship
might not be the best thing. I told him that I'll
always want to be close friends with him, but that
I'm not sure about the rest of it. I could tell by
his response that he was a little hurt. But he
said he understood. I hope so.

BURNING BRIDGES
along the road
you miss a turn
you go too far
you end up burned
one wrong choice
you lose your way
you continue on
when you should stay
without a compass
you stub your toe
you don't recall
the way to go

don't burn the bridge
that you must cross
when you realize
all that's lost
you can go back
there's time to turn
God can restore
the bridge that burned
cm

Thursday, October 7

(HANGIN' IN ALBUQUERQUE)

We've had a pretty quiet week, all things considered. It's been a good chance to get caught up on things like schoolwork and rest and also e-mail. It's funny to think that of all the e-mail I get—and it's really quite a lot these days since everyone I know seems to want to write to a "rock star"—I've discovered that I look forward to the ones from my dad the most.

This has taken me completely by surprise. I mean, I realize I'm only sixteen, and by all rights I should still be living at home and begging to stay out later than my ten o'clock curfew. But I also know that I think of myself as older somehow—like I'm ready to be independent and on my own. And I am, sort of. It's also true that I hadn't felt terribly close to my parents during

the past few years, which was mostly my fault. I
was so consumed with being a rebel that I thought
my parents were hopelessly lame, and I went out
of my way to avoid having a relationship with
them at all.

Now I'm finding that I feel bad for the time I
wasted, and it makes me miss my parents. I can
tell my dad really misses me, and that feels kind
of cool. He says my mom misses me too, and I don't
think he'd lie about something like that. But she
doesn't do e-mail, and I've only talked to her a
couple of times on the phone. So it's hard to say.
But that's okay. I accept that Mom and I are just
two very different people. I love her anyway, and
I know she loves me.

Speaking of parents and families, we all just
got this great idea. We've decided to see if we can
fly our parents out to Dallas on October 23. We're
having a pretty big concert that night, and we
thought it'd be fun to have them come and see us
and stay a couple nights at the hotel. We asked
Willy to check into this—and see if we can afford
it. Because despite what people may think, we do
live within a budget. Oh, sure, we all have more
money than we could make working at the coffee-
house or McDonald's, but we're certainly not
millionaires.

Anyway, it's fun to think of having them all
come out. Not so much that I want to impress them

with our new status of "stardom," which is really an overstatement, but I would like them to see us opening for Iron Cross. That, I feel, is quite an accomplishment. And I want them to meet the guys in the band.

OLD HOLDS
family ties
sing to me
stubborn lies
cling to me
peel away
start again
help me stay
free from sin
learn to love
how to live
God above
help me forgive
cm

Friday, October 8
(SEEING SANTA FE)

Somehow we got our schedules a bit confused (my fault I'm sure), and both Iron Cross and Redemption showed up at the same time to practice this afternoon. We're sharing the same practice room at the hotel, getting ready for our concert tomorrow night. Anyway, the guys were real sweet about it and actually invited us to a little jam session with them.

It was so cool. Just jamming with Iron Cross. Talk about stoked. And our combined sound wasn't half bad either. Not that we'll be taking it to the stage anytime soon. Or ever, for that matter. But it was fun.

After we finished up, we hung in the practice room for a while. We were trying to think of something fun to do but were having a hard time agreeing on anything. Some of us wanted to do something outdoors, and others (like Allie and Laura and Brett) seemed content to go mall hopping. Finally, we decided to split up, and I ended up going with Jeremy and Isaiah. Our plan was to drive up to Santa Fe, which we figured would take about an hour.

We got into the rental car, this black Mustang convertible that the guys had been sharing, and we headed up the highway. Jeremy was the driver, and I offered to sit in back since I'm shorter and the legroom's a little cramped back there— besides, it seemed right. The plan was to just stop wherever we wanted along the way.

Well, the country was drop-dead gorgeous and we stopped a lot. The rugged mountains and pine trees were stunning, the air was clean and clear, and the sky was this amazing jewel-tone shade of blue. It became quite obvious that Jeremy was a real nature freak. Anyway, that's what Isaiah calls him.

"Jeremy just goes nuts over things like trees and birds and stuff," Isaiah said after Jeremy had pulled over to better investigate what he thought was an eagle.

"I think that's cool," I admitted. "Nature can be pretty inspiring."

Jeremy smiled. "Yeah, we poets need to stick together."

I think that's one of the nicest compliments I've ever had. But I'm not sure if I even said thank you or not.

We finally made it to Santa Fe and went to this cool Mexican restaurant for dinner. The building was made out of adobe and looked like it was about a hundred years old. We sat outside on a terra-cotta patio, under lots of festive, colorful lanterns. They even had live music (a marimba band), and I honestly felt like I was in some old cheesy Hollywood movie. Only it was totally fun. And surprisingly, I found myself really opening up to these guys.

"I'm just not that comfortable with the one-on-one stuff," I told them as we started our dessert. "You know, signing autographs and talking with strangers who act like you're some kind of superstar."

"Man, that's the best part." Isaiah laughed then pointed his finger at Jeremy. "Although not everyone thinks so."

Jeremy smiled. "I'm not that comfortable with it either."

"Really?" I studied this confident-looking young man and wondered how that could possibly be true.

He nodded. "I'm fine up there onstage, Chloe, but when I'm face-to-face with a fan, I get a little unnerved."

"Yes!" Relief washed over me. "That's exactly how I feel. But Allie and Laura seem perfectly fine with it. I thought I was just weird."

"Well, welcome to the club," said Jeremy.

"Does it get any better?" I asked.

He shrugged. "Sometimes I think it does. After all, we've been doing this for five years. But then there are times when I'd like to go climb in a hole too."

"Yeah," said Isaiah. "We have to keep our eye on him."

"Do you have any suggestions?" I looked at Jeremy hopefully. "Any magical answers?"

He laughed. "I wish. Mostly I try to put the whole thing into God's hands and trust Him. But I also think it's therapeutic to just keep thrusting yourself out there. It's like facing your fears."

I sighed. "I suppose. But sometimes it's overwhelming."

"I know. I've read some on social anxiety disorders."

"Is that what this is?" I asked. "Does it really have a name?"

"Man, they have names for everything," said Isaiah. "You could be afraid of sneezing in crowds, and the shrinks would give it a name."

"Sometimes it helps to have a name attached. It helps you to know what you're dealing with," said Jeremy. "Sure, it doesn't solve the problem, but it makes you realize that you're not alone and there might be ways to cope with it better."

I smiled. "I have to admit, it makes me feel better knowing that you struggle with it and that it's something real—not just in my head, you know?"

Jeremy nodded. "I know."

Then we started talking about music again, critiquing the marimba band and sharing some of the things that inspire us. It was so cool just hanging with these guys tonight. And on the way home, riding in the backseat of the convertible with the top down and knowing that the guys in the front seat are members of the best band in the country...well, it was almost more than my little pea brain could take in.

And to be perfectly honest, it was sort of

romantic too. I can't believe I just admitted this.
It's something I could only say in the privacy of
my diary. No way would I want anyone besides God
to know—and there's no hiding it from Him. But
I'd freak if Allie or Laura—and definitely
Jeremy—had any idea of how I feel right now.

But the truth is, I'm afraid that I'm getting a
real crush on Jeremy. Okay, I know this guy's way
older than me, and in a way that makes it seem
okay. It's as if he's so unattainable that it's safe.
Besides, he treats me like his kid sister. And
that's okay too. Really. It makes me feel like I can
hang with him without getting all worried that
anything could go sideways. And I just like being
with him. I like talking about music and lyrics
and life and God with him. Now, is there anything
wrong with that?

KEEP ME SAFE
watch your step
and guard your heart
you think you heard
the music start
but take it easy
don't let go
keep your cool
don't let it show
keep me safe, Lord,
hold my hand

sometimes i don't
understand
You know my heart
belongs to You
keep it safe
my whole life through
cm

Ten

Wednesday, October 13

(ORDINARY DAY IN EL PASO)

Saturday's concert in Santa Fe was great. In my humble opinion both bands totally rocked. The crowd seemed to agree, and Eric said that Redemption was the perfect complement to Iron Cross.

"I think these two bands could have a really bright future together," he told Willy the next morning as we were getting ready to head out. "The big boys at Omega like what they're hearing. And Iron Cross is pleased too."

"What went wrong with the last band who toured with them?" asked Willy.

"Spirit Walkers?" Eric shook his head. "It's kind of a long story, but the nutshell version is they fell apart."

Willy nodded as he loaded the last of the drum kit into the storage bin. "Yeah, that's usually the case."

Eric smiled as he glanced over to where Allie and I were lurking and eavesdropping. Okay, we were just listening. "But that's not going to happen with Redemption. Is it, ladies?"

"No way," Allie said with full confidence.

"Not as long as God's holding us together," I added. But I can't deny that hearing about another band falling apart ran a slight chill down my spine.

"That's the attitude." Eric patted me on the back. "All things are possible through God, right?"

I nodded.

"See you in Dallas then." He grinned. "Oh, by the way, I probably shouldn't tell you this, but a couple of the bigwigs are flying out with me for the Dallas concert. Hopefully you guys will be hot that night."

"I'm sure we'll do our best," I assured him. "We've got family coming to that concert."

"Great. It'll be a good one for everybody then."

So we've been really getting in the practice time this week. Willy and I both agree that we need to make up for lost time—specifically for our little lull when Laura wasn't up to speed. I think we're sounding better and better, and I've been able to introduce a couple new songs. My two favorite parts of this tour are practicing and performing—well, and getting to know the members of Iron Cross—but I'm trying to handle the publicity stuff better too.

Now that our CD is officially released, we're expected to make appearances at the major

Christian bookstores along the way. I have to say this is stretching me—a lot. Still, I remind myself that Jeremy struggles with the same thing. Iron Cross isn't expected to make as many appearances as we do since their music literally flies off the shelf. I know this is because they've done this already. They've paid their dues.

I don't know what I'd do if Allie and Laura weren't so comfortable with this part of the business. Sometimes it feels as if they're holding me up and pulling me through these times. But I guess that's okay. It's like we've all got our gifts. And while I'm gifted at the creative end, I need some serious help with the rest. And that's probably a good thing.

HANDS AND FEET
we are all just pieces
elbows, feet, and toes
each one has a purpose
ears and eyes and nose
one without the other
what good does it do?
hands without the fingers
not much use, it's true
but we're all connected
Jesus is the head
the heartbeat comes from heaven
when it's done and said

> only God unites us
> makes us work together
> giving Him the glory
> today until forever
>
> cm

Sunday, October 17

(DAY OF REST IN DALLAS)

We have a concert in Fort Worth on Tuesday, then we practice until the big event in Dallas on Saturday. Willy took us to church this morning. An old music friend of his is the pastor there, and Willy had specifically asked his buddy not to mention that we (Redemption) were visiting his church. Not that anyone would care since we haven't done a concert in their area yet, and it's not like we're that well-known. But I must admit, it was a relief to go someplace without everyone knowing who we were or making a big deal about us. I felt like I could actually breathe. Not to mention worship. It's not that I can't worship God when people are glancing at me from down the pew, and I actually believe that I do worship God when I'm onstage performing, but it's different somehow. I guess I miss the kind of worship I was able to participate in back home, back when I was just a member of an ordinary congregation.

Sometimes it scares me to think that I may never get back to that ordinary sort of life. It's not that I don't want Redemption to do well and even become famous. In some ways I do. Especially when it comes to performing my music and having it appreciated by the audiences. But still, there's a price you must pay. Sometimes I wonder how willing I really am to pay it. And I suppose that scares me.

PRICE OF FAME

we want it all, or so we say
but what gets lost along the way?
along the road to riches, fame
we know we'll never be the same
we start like this, but then we change
our lives completely rearrange
how can we add up what it cost?
how do we measure what is lost?
what is the price, what is our fate?
can we turn back, is it too late?
is this the way we want to live?
is this the best that we can give?
there is the One who gave His all
He paid the price, He took the fall
for all He gave, what did He earn?
what did they pay Him in return?
and so i'll give my everything
each day i live, each time i sing
but not for wealth and not for fame
i'll give to glorify His name

cm

Thursday, October 21

(DOWN AND OUT IN DALLAS)

Dallas is one of the wealthiest cities in the United States, or so I've been told. But here's what I've noticed—and to be fair, I've noticed this in every big city we've been through—I've seen homeless people everywhere. I don't mean everywhere, as in on every street. But I've seen them in every city. Sometimes they're panhandling by the hotels we stay in. Or sometimes you just see them clustered on a corner, and you can tell they're homeless by their clothes and their hangdog expressions. At least I can.

I'm sure it's easy for some people to miss them. Laura and Allie don't really seem to notice them at all. I know this for a fact because I've mentioned this to them several times, and they both act as if I'm overreacting or imagining things. But the truth is, I seem to see them everywhere. I remind myself of that kid in "The Sixth Sense" who said, "I see dead people." Except I see homeless people. And I know they're not invisible. But that's how it feels sometimes. It's like no one else even sees them.

And that really bothers me. I think it bothers me even more because so many of them seem to be about my age or thereabouts. What are they doing on the streets? They look perfectly miserable to me. Why don't they just go home? Okay, I'm not stupid, and I know it's not that simple. Life never is. But seeing these kids has got me thinking about my oldest brother, Caleb. I wonder if he's hanging out on the streets like that, and that cuts deep into my heart.

Okay, this is what I remember about Caleb. He was kind and gentle and had the most beautiful brown eyes. He liked playing soccer in the back-yard with me and helping me with homework, and I don't remember him ever teasing me or being mean. I would never admit this to anyone, but as a kid I think I loved Caleb more than Josh. Caleb is about two and half years older than Josh, which makes him almost twenty-four now. I haven't seen him for about three years, and whenever I think of him I get extremely sad. And for that reason I suppose I try not to think of him too much, although I do pray for him daily.

The last time I saw Caleb was when he came home for Christmas, back when I was thirteen—just a year before I went through my rebellious streak. Anyway, by then Caleb had been in college for about a year, and I'd noticed how much he'd changed. He'd gone off looking like the Caleb I'd always known—clean-cut and athletic—but he returned with scraggly hair and looking a little gnarly around the edges.

My parents didn't realize it was drugs to start

with. But when he got suspended from school for smoking grass and consequently lost his football scholarship, they both got very upset. My dad told him to get a job and save up his own college tuition money. And I thought that was what he'd been doing all that year.

But when Caleb came home for Christmas the following year, we all knew something was really wrong. It's as if he'd undergone a complete personality change—he looked burnt-out, hardly smiled, and even seemed to be a little paranoid every time the phone rang or someone came to the door. It was weird. Finally, on Christmas Eve, he asked my parents to loan him some money.

"I need to get a car," he explained. "So I can get a good job, you know, and start saving for college."

"Look, Caleb," I overheard Dad tell him. "We've sent you money in the past. You always say you're going to use it to get clothes for job interviews or for going back to school or something worthwhile. Then it's always the same old story: The next thing we know you're broke and jobless. Nothing ever changes with you."

"Hey, it's not easy—"

"That's right! Doing drugs is not easy. It's not easy on anyone."

A few more words were exchanged, and then Caleb stormed out of there, promising to never come back. As a result, it was not a happy

Christmas that year. I think it had a pretty negative impact on everyone in our family. My dad started working longer hours; my mom seemed more edgy and depressed. Josh got into drinking and partying about that same time, and it wasn't too much later that I went into my dark period.

Oh, I'm not blaming all this on Caleb. It's just the way life happened for the Miller family. And if anything, I feel really sorry for Caleb. I hated the way my parents dealt with him. Naturally, they called it "tough love," but it seemed more like "tough luck" to me. My dad made it perfectly clear to Caleb that as long as he was into drugs, he was not welcome in our home.

Okay, I can sort of understand that, but where did that mean Caleb could go? Where would he find help? On the streets? That's where I envision him sometimes. It's not an image I'm comfortable with, but it's probably a real possibility. So every time I see a guy in his twenties with shaggy brown hair and dark soulful eyes, I have to look twice. And I wonder, could that be him? Could that be my brother Caleb? Because I have no idea where he is, or worse yet, if he's even still alive. I can't even describe how much it hurts to think of this. Like a dull knife twisting inside my gut. But every time I feel it, I pray for him.

RESCUE HIM

on the streets, down and out
burnt and broke and full of doubt
out of luck and out of time
buddy, could you spare a dime?
sagging spirits, hopeless eyes
bum a buck with see-through lies
looking down, a sideways glance
afraid to try, to take a chance
God, reach out Your loving hand
help him see and understand
Your love can give a clean, fresh start
Your love can fill an empty heart
Your love can make his life brand new
help him to give his heart to You.

amen

Eleven

Saturday, October 23

(HANGIN' WITH THE FAM)

Tonight's concert felt like I was living my happiest fantasy. But let me back up a bit. Josh and my parents and Laura's parents and brother all arrived in Dallas this afternoon. We met them at the airport in a stretch limo, no less, and took them out for an early dinner. Our treat, of course. Actually, the whole weekend was our treat. Guess that's one of the perks of this biz—you actually have enough money to do some cool things.

I still can't believe how thrilled I was to see my family. I think it surprised them too. I hugged each of them long and hard. Even my mom. She was actually wiping tears from her eyes when I finally let go. That was cool.

"You look older, Chloe," she said as she assessed my outfit. I'd gone to special effort to put on something a little more traditional than my usual urban "trash," as my mom would call it. I think she appreciated it.

"You guys look great," I told them. "I can't believe how much I've missed you."

Josh grinned. "I know exactly what you mean.

You don't appreciate the old fogies until you
leave home."

We had to hurry a bit through dinner, but no
one seemed to mind. Then we took them back to the
hotel, where Laura and I had booked our parents
some very nice suites, as well as a room for Josh
and Laura's brother, James. And again, they
seemed suitably impressed. I'm not sure why this
means so much to me, but for some reason it does.
Maybe it has to do with the times that my mom sort
of pooh-poohed the whole music thing, like it
wasn't such a big deal. But I could tell by her
expression that her thoughts on this may have
changed some since then.

As usual, we had to get to the auditorium
early, but we had prearranged another limo to
pick up our families as well as front-row seats
for the concert.

I felt more excited and nervous than usual as
we went onto the stage. But the audience was
enthusiastic, and I started to relax as soon as I
had the mike in my hand.

"Hey, y'all" I yelled, imitating their Texan
drawl. "It's great to be down here in the Lone Star
State. Praise God for Texas!" Naturally this
brought a big applause. "And tonight is a big
night for Redemption. As y'all know we're pretty
new to the music scene. And this is the first time
our folks have been out to see us perform as

warm-up for Iron Cross, only the hottest band in Christian music." Again the crowd went wild. It's amazing how just saying the name "Iron Cross" can get a crowd jazzed.

I pointed down to the front row where our families were seated. "I hope you'll welcome our families here tonight. And with God's help and grace, we'll give you the best music we've got in us!" Then we started to play. And we rocked! And the crowd rocked! And I honestly believe it was the best concert we've ever given. Even Jeremy said so when he came out onto the stage and thanked us in front of the totally stoked crowd.

"Are these girls great or what?" he asked the crowd, and they clapped and cheered even louder. "I keep telling them that it won't be long before we're opening for them." This brought good-humored laughter and more applause. Then we went down and sat with our families for the rest of the concert. Josh leaned over and looked me in the eye.

"You are totally amazing, sis!"

I'm sure my face was just one great big smile by then. "Thanks."

After the concert we took our families backstage to meet Iron Cross. "That Jeremy really has his head together," my dad said afterward when we all met at the hotel restaurant for a late night dessert.

"Yeah," I agreed. "He's pretty cool."

"He said some nice things about you too." Dad winked at me.

I managed to maintain a calm exterior. "Well, he's a gracious guy." Now I have absolutely no intention of revealing to anyone that I have feelings for this guy. Besides, I keep telling myself, it's a schoolgirl crush that will pass in time.

"Don't you want to know what he said?" demanded Allie.

I just shrugged.

My dad smiled at Allie. "He said that I should be proud of my daughter, that she's not only a talented musician but a fine person too."

Allie smirked at me. "I guess that's true."

"Gee, thanks," I told her.

"It's just so unbelievable," James said suddenly.

"What?" asked Laura.

"That you girls—our baby sisters—are out here playing music with a group like Iron Cross."

Laura frowned. "What do you mean? Don't you think we're good enough?"

He laughed. "Obviously you're good enough. You guys are fantastic." Then he shook his head. "But it's still unbelievable."

"I know what you mean," said Josh. "It feels weird to be shown up by your kid sister."

"Hey, we all have our gifts," I told them.

"There are things you guys can do that we'll never be good at. Like sports," I added. "You both are really great athletes."

"Yeah, but we'll never make the kind of money you guys are making with sports."

"It's not all about the money," I said. "And who knows how long this ride will last anyway."

"That's right," added Willy. "The music industry is a finicky business. Things can change at the drop of a hat."

"So you better enjoy it while it's here." My dad raised his soda glass as if to toast us. "And here's to three incredibly talented girls and what appears to be a very bright future!"

All in all, it was a nearly perfect day. Unfortunately, I had to go and spoil things as my parents and I were going up in the elevator together. They had decided to turn in early, and I wanted to see them to their room.

"I've been thinking about Caleb a lot lately," I said as soon as the elevator started going up.

Dad cleared his throat. "Why's that, pumpkin?"

"Well, I see all these down-and-out homeless kids in every city and—"

"Caleb has made his choices," my dad interrupted.

"But I keep wondering if he's okay."

My mom sniffed, and I turned to see that her

eyes were filling with tears, but she didn't say anything.

"I just wonder if there's anything I can do to—"

"Chloe, I know that you love Caleb, and now that you've got money, I'm sure it would seem like a good idea to help him. But believe me, money is not what Caleb needs."

"I just wondered if you ever hear from him," I continued even though I could tell I was upsetting my parents. "I think about him sometimes, in the middle of the night, and I get so worried and scared for him. Of course, I pray for him, but I just wonder if there's something more—"

"Praying might be the best thing you can do for him," Dad said as the elevator stopped on their floor.

I turned to look at my mom. "Do you know where he is?"

She pressed her lips together and looked at my dad.

"Honey," Dad put his hand on my arm, "I know you only have Caleb's best interests at heart. And that's good. But I think you'd be wise to avoid him. At least until he's ready to make some serious changes in his lifestyle."

Mom sighed then hugged me. "I'm so proud of you, Chloe."

I nodded and swallowed hard. I appreciated her words, but I was so focused on Caleb that I didn't completely absorb the meaning until I was back in my room. And it was sweet of her to say that. Really. Just the same, I would've rather have heard what's going on with Caleb. I'm sure they must know where he lives. Maybe I'll ask Josh about it tomorrow.

SOMETHING'S MISSING
here we are just sittin' 'round
laughing, joking, happy sound
family time with smiling faces
all of us are in our places
but something's missing, someone's gone
something about this feels all wrong
on the outside looking in
i wish that he'd come back again
misfit brother, caring eyes
when will you finally realize
you are loved just as you are
by the Man who bore your scars?
if you'd listen, i could tell
that you're loved by me as well
and i'd tell you more things too
my sweet brother, where are you?
cm

Tuesday, October 26

(BIRTHDAY ON THE ROAD)

It was a little tricky planning a birthday party for Laura since we were driving to Tulsa today, but somehow we managed to pull it off. First, we all pretended like we'd forgotten it was her birthday this morning. I could tell that she was a little ticked about it, but she kept her thoughts to herself.

After breakfast, Allie took our gifts and stuff and rode with Willy so they could set things up. Meanwhile, Rosy pretended to take a "shortcut," buying time for Willy and Allie so they could get there ahead of us.

Our destination was a tiny town named Mitchell—just like Laura's last name. This was Rosy's idea since she's the one who knows where everything is. The plan was for Rosy to pretend to be lost. A real stretch because that woman seems to have a road map imprinted into her brain. She always knows where we are and when we're going to get to our destination.

"I thought this would take us straight up to Tulsa," she announced as we meandered down a country road. "Guess I was wrong."

Laura didn't even look up from her schoolwork, but Elise winked at me.

"Maybe you should call Willy and ask him for some directions," I said from my spot at the table.

"Yeah, guess I'll do that. Don't recall ever being lost before."

I could hear her talking on the phone but sounding more confused than ever. Finally she said, "I think I'll just stop in the next town and ask for directions."

"Mitchell," I said as we drove within the city limits.

"Huh?" Laura looked up.

"The town," I told her. "It's called Mitchell."

She just nodded as if she could care less.

"Population 154," I said as Rosy slowed down.

"I'm gonna stop at this café and ask for directions," she called back to us. "You guys want anything?"

Elise took Davie by the hand. "Yeah, I think I'll get Davie something."

"I want a soda," I said. "You coming, Laura?"

She just shook her head.

Now we had expected this might happen. So we got out and went in without her. We figured we could make sure everything was all ready.

Willy and Allie had the little café completely decorated with balloons and crepe paper and flowers. The cake and the gifts were on a table, and the owner of the restaurant looked pleased to have our business. Allie later told me that they had to pay him extra.

Then I went back to the bus to get Laura. I

already knew what I would say. Laura has this funky old collection of salt and pepper shakers that her great-grandma left to her. She has them on shelves in her bedroom. And we all know that she has a weakness for buying a new set when she discovers something unique.

"You gotta come in here and see their salt and pepper shakers," I told her. "They must have a hundred of them."

"Really?" Her dark eyes lit up and she set aside her laptop.

Now I felt a little bad, except that I knew my gift contained several sets I know she's been wanting for her collection.

"Yeah, come on."

Well, to say she was surprised would be a complete understatement. She was so shocked that she began to shake and cry. A little un-Laura-like but sweet. Then we all hugged her, and it took her three attempts to blow out all seventeen candles.

It was a fun little break in our otherwise mundane day. Several locals were looking on with curiosity, and when they discovered (from the owner) that we were a real band, they came over and asked for our autographs. I'm sure they'd never heard of us before, but we signed for them just the same. And Willy even gave the café owner a CD.

All in all, it was a good party, and I think
Laura really appreciated it. It felt good to make
her feel special. For some reason this tour has
seemed harder on her than any of us expected. So
Allie and I made a pact to go out of our way to
make Laura happier.

OUR TIMES
happy days and holidays
all days belong to You
the Alpha and Omega
the One who sees us through
time can be so fleeting
it's hard to understand
hours, seconds, minutes
all resting in Your hand
present, past, and future
we can't control the flow
of months and years and decades
but here's one thing we know
God can measure out our lives
to live in certainty
when we put all trust in Him
we've all eternity
cm

Twelve

Thursday, October 28

(OK IN OKLAHOMA)

It's hard to believe that we've been opening for Iron Cross for more than a month now. Man, how the time flies. I just looked at our concert schedule and discovered that we only have ten concerts left on this leg of our tour. Then we go home for Christmas break. Elise has really been riding us hard on our schoolwork. I think this has more to do with Allie than Laura and me, but I suppose we've all gotten a little lazy, or "unmotivated," as Elise so kindly puts it.

"You girls have to keep your grades up," she said this morning as we were heading toward Oklahoma City. "Or else they might replace me as your chaperone."

"Oh, Mom. They won't do that."

"Oh, yes, they will." Elise helped Davie open up the tin that holds his crayons. "You girls know I don't have any teaching credentials. Good grief, I only completed two years of college before I quit to get married." She shook her head. "Now, if that wasn't one of the stupidest moves of my life."

"You could go back to college," said Allie. "We could probably afford it now."

Elise laughed. "Hey, maybe you and I could go to college together."

Allie shook her head. "No way. I don't even want to go to college."

"Allie!" Laura scowled at her from across the table where she was writing a paper for her economics class. "You've got to go to college."

"Why?"

"To further your education, stupid."

Allie stuck her chin out. "Who you calling stupid?"

Laura looked down. "Sorry, that wasn't too cool. But get real, Allie. We all have to go to college. Right, Elise?"

"That'd be my vote. I've always been sorry that I quit."

"But what about our music?" I asked. "How do we keep Redemption alive and go to college at the same time?"

Laura shrugged. "Who knows what will happen by then, Chloe. All I know is that I made a promise to my parents that I would go to college, and I intend to keep it."

Allie winked at me. "I guess we'll have to start looking around for another bass player."

"Whad'ya mean?" Laura looked up with a hurt expression.

"Well, if you're going to bail on us—"

"I never said—"

"All right, all right," Elise interrupted. "Whether or when you girls go to college does not have to be determined today. The fact is, none of you will get accepted into college if you don't do your schoolwork. So I am now imposing silence on the bus until we get to Oklahoma City. Understand?"

"Amen!" called Rosy from her driver's seat. "You girls' fighting is wearing thin on my nerves."

So we quietly did our schoolwork, and the next thing I knew we were driving through Oklahoma City and parking in front of our hotel. As we were unloading I felt a tap on my shoulder. A guy not much older than me, I'd guess, stood beside me, smiling in a hopeful way. I could tell right away that this guy lived on the streets. His hands were grimy and his clothes were tattered and shabby.

"Hey, can you spare me a buck or two? I haven't eaten in days."

I fished in my pocket for a wadded-up five dollar bill and held it out to him. "Here you go," I said, relieved that I could finally help out a homeless person.

His eyes grew wide and his smile broadened to reveal a set of uneven and yellowed teeth. "Wow, thanks. Thanks a lot!"

I felt really good as he walked away. It would be so cool if someone did something like this for my brother Caleb.

"Hey, Chloe," Willy said as he loaded an amp onto the luggage cart.

"Yeah?" I went over to give him a hand.

"Did you just give that guy some money?"

"He looked as if he really needed it."

"Uh-huh." Willy nodded as he set another bag onto the nearly full cart. Then he stood up and looked at me. "What do you think he's going to do with that money?"

"Hopefully get himself something to eat."

Willy frowned. "Chances are that's not what it'll go for."

"Whad'ya mean?"

"I know you gave him the money out of the kindness of your heart, Chloe, but most of the time when people are sp'anging—"

"What's that?" I ran the strange word that rhymes with "changing" through my head.

"'Sp'ange' is slang for 'panhandling,' short for 'spare change.' You know, got any spare change?"

"Oh."

"Anyway, most of the folks that are sp'anging on the streets are doing drugs, Chloe. And when you give them money, it's as good as buying them dope."

"But he said he was hungry."

"Yeah, he probably was. But most of these guys would rather buy dope than food."

I frowned. "Do you really think he's going to buy drugs with that money?"

Willy shrugged. "It's a fair guess. Of course, he'll have to sp'ange around until he gets enough to buy a hit of whatever his substance of abuse is. But I'll bet that's where your money goes." He set another bag on the cart. "I remember how much money I wasted on my LSD habit, back in the old days."

"That's right," I said as I remembered how Willy used to be an acid freak before he became a Jesus freak (his own words).

"I used to wish for that money back, but now I'm just thankful I escaped that crud altogether. What a hopeless life. And believe me, I feel sorry for the guys on the street. Just the same, I wouldn't be handing out money to them, Chloe."

I sighed. "Well, now I feel totally stupid. I only wanted to help him get something to eat."

"I know, Chloe. Don't beat yourself up over it. And like all things, you can always pray and ask God to help you know what to do in situations like this. I just thought you should understand how it really is out here on the streets."

We had everything unloaded by then, and we helped wheel the carts into the hotel. I wanted to tell Willy about Caleb and how worried I get for him, but it didn't really seem like good timing. Still, I think I will sometime. I know he'll understand. I had tried to bring up the subject with Josh before they flew out last Sunday, but it seemed as though he didn't really want to talk about it.

"I don't know what to tell you, Chloe," he said. "Caleb is living his own life on his own terms. Until he surrenders himself to God, I don't see how anything is going to change. Still, we need to keep praying."

"I know. And I do pray. I just wish we could do something more."

Josh just shrugged. "I don't know what it would be. Honestly, I don't even know where Caleb is these days."

But after "helping" that guy on the street, I'm questioning myself. What I thought was helping might not be helpful at all. I may have just enabled someone to continue in their dead-end lifestyle. Still, I'm praying for the guy with the bad teeth, asking God to redeem my mistake. I just wish life didn't have to be so confusing.

HOW DOES IT GO?
you think you're doing good
until you find it's bad
you feel all warm and happy

and then you get all sad
you wanna help your neighbor
and give him something good
instead you give him drugs
when what he needs is food
tell me how You do it, God
how does this whole thing go?
how're you s'posed to lend a hand?
how are you s'posed to know?
God, there must be ways to help
ways so that we can share
God, there must be things to do
things to show we care
cm

Tuesday, November 2

(REACHING OUT IN LITTLE ROCK)

You've got questions; God's got answers. And when
I asked Him to help me come up with a way to help
homeless people, He gave me an idea. Okay, it's
just a very small idea, a tiny gesture, but I think
it's pretty cool.

After my talk with Willy about the perils of
giving money to sp'angers, I decided to head over
to McDonald's for lunch. Naturally, Allie (queen
of the junk food junkies) wanted to come along.
Laura said she wasn't hungry. Anyway, after I
ordered a Big Mac and a soda, I also bought fifty

bucks' worth of gift certificates.

"What's up with that?" asked Allie. "You doing your Christmas shopping early?"

I smiled. "Sort of."

"No, seriously," she said as she fingered the stack of packets. "What are you gonna do with all those?"

"Well, a guy sp'anged me—"

Allie's eyes grew wide with alarm. "What? Did you get hurt?"

I laughed. "'Sp'ange' is slang for 'spare change.'"

"Huh?"

"A homeless guy asked me for some money at the hotel, and I gave him a five—"

"That's cool." Allie dipped a fry in ketchup. "Isn't it great that we have enough money to help people out?" She slowly shook her head. "Man, I can remember hard times when I was so broke that I was ready to go sp'anging myself." She smiled with satisfaction. I'm not sure if it was over using her new word or the idea that she didn't have to beg for money anymore.

"Yeah, well, Willy said that by giving that guy money, I was in essence buying him dope."

"No way." Allie frowned. "You wouldn't do that, Chloe."

"Not intentionally. But Willy made a good point."

She eyed my stack of certificates. "Aha. I think I gotcha. Are you going to give those away?"

I smiled. "Yep."

"Hey, I wanna get some too. This could be fun."

So after we finished eating, Allie went up and got several booklets of her own.

Then sure enough, we were barely on the street when a girl with a sad expression approached us. I suspected by the look in her eye that she wanted to ask for money. Her hair looked ratty beneath her black stocking cap, and her nylon parka was crusty with dirt.

"Can you spare some change for a cup of coffee?" she asked in a timid voice.

"We can do better than that," offered Allie. Then she turned and looked at me, worried I'm sure that she was stealing the show.

I nodded. "Go ahead."

Allie pulled out a pack of certificates, tore out several dollars' worth, and handed them to the girl. "Here."

The girl looked kind of surprised. It was hard to tell if she was happy or disappointed.

"Look," said Allie. "You probably need a meal. Go over to McDonald's and get yourself something to eat, okay?"

She nodded. "Yeah, okay."

"And God bless you." I said.

"Yeah," said Allie with a smile. "God bless

you. And remember Jesus is the way. Call on Him and He'll answer."

The girl studied us as she slowly backed away. I'm not sure if she thought we were nuts or religious fanatics or what, but hopefully God used us.

We were about a block from the hotel when Allie spotted a guy coming our direction. "Hey, Chloe," she said in undertones, "that guy looks like he might be homeless too. Ya think he's going to sp'ange us?"

I had to smile. "Maybe."

"Well, you go ahead and do it this time."

I laughed. "Yeah, sure, whatever."

And sure enough, by the time he reached us, he had his hand out. "Can you help me out?" His eyes looked flat and slightly glazed, his cheeks hollowed from hunger. "Got any spare change?"

So I whipped out my McDonald's coupons, and instead of tearing out some pages I handed him a whole booklet. "Here you go," I told him as I peered into his eyes. "And God bless you."

Again, we got the curious look. I'm still not sure if he was disappointed or just surprised, but he did say thank you.

"And don't forget," called Allie as he was walking away. "Jesus is the only One who can set you free."

"And when He sets you free, you'll be free indeed," I called out after her.

"You're sure generous," Allie told me as we headed into the hotel.

"Guess I better really stock up on these."

So that's our plan. And when Laura found out, she decided to do the same. I told them that we should keep what we're doing quiet like the way Jesus says to do your good works in secret so your Heavenly Father can reward you. We don't need the whole world to know that Redemption and McDonald's are working in cahoots to feed the homeless. But at the same time, I'm thinking this is just the beginning. There must be other ways to help out too. And I'm going to ask God to show me. In the meantime, I'm handing out Mickey D-bucks to every sp'anger I meet. And it's pretty fun!

A SMALL THING
Mickey D-bucks and coffee cups
doesn't take so very much
to reach out, lend a hand
let them know we understand
Jesus fed the hungry crowd
broke the bread, prayed aloud
loaves and fishes, multiplied
hungry hearts were satisfied
cm

Thirteen

Sunday, November 7

(WALKING IN MEMPHIS)

It's a quiet day. We went to church in Memphis this morning, after performing last night, and then hit the road again. I must admit to feeling a little road weary. I think we're all tired and looking forward to Thanksgiving break in a couple of weeks. We get to go home for four days of a blissful break.

One of the toughest things about this concert tour is constantly being with people. While we're on the bus there is no getting away from the others. At the hotels there are always people around. But the concerts are the worst. Sometimes I feel almost claustrophobic from being surrounded by people. I've even imagined myself totally flipping out and screaming, "Leave me alone!" as the fans clamor around, asking for autographs. I know it's totally ungracious on my part, but it's how I feel.

I guess I never realized how much I enjoy being alone at times. But it's hard to get quiet times like that on the road. Oh sure, we all have our quiet times in the morning, but we do it within the confines of the bus. And of course, I can take a little walk when we stop for gas or a break, but I'm always on a short leash. When I go home for Thanksgiving, I think I'll spend a whole day in the cemetery, just enjoying the silence up there. I'm sure that sounds weird to some people, but it sounds like a welcome relief to me.

I got an interesting e-mail from Cesar today. We still write each other, but not as much as before. He seems okay with the "just being friends" thing now. Very okay. At first I'd thought he was hurt, but it seems he's moved right along with his life. I'm impressed with how much he's growing spiritually. He's involved in a guys Bible study and working with a ministry that reaches out to middle school kids. He's even gotten his little sister Abril involved. But here's what really blew me away.

"I just read this book about dating," he wrote in his e-mail. "It's written by a guy named Josh Harris and called 'I Kissed Dating Goodbye.' Anyway, the premise is that dating only leads to problems. At first I was pretty skeptical, but the more I read, the more I agreed with the author. And I can understand this whole thing from firsthand experience. So brace yourself, Chloe, but I've decided to kiss dating good-bye too."

Well, I was a little surprised by this. In fact, I wasn't entirely sure if he meant he was "kissing

me good-bye" too, although we'd already agreed
to continue our relationship as "just friends," so
I guess it shouldn't matter. But somehow seeing
those words in print felt like a small slap in my
face. All right, I know I'm being terribly self-
centered and shallow and immature, but it's how I
felt.

Still, it's not as if I haven't heard this kind
of philosophy before. After all, this is what
Caitlin truly believes. And I've seen my own
brother devastated by dating. Although, in
Caitlin's defense, they seem to be getting along
better than ever these days, but only as friends.
I guess Cesar's note just caught me a little off
guard. To be perfectly honest, I think I enjoyed
the idea of Cesar being slightly in love with me.
Oh, what a selfish little fool I am.

Because the rest of the truth is, I still have a
crush on Jeremy. Oh, sure, I do a fantastic job of
keeping it under wraps. Unlike Allie who actually practices writing her name as "Mrs. Brett
James" and will launch into spontaneous discus-
sions about how smart Brett is, how good he is on
drums, and she can go on and on about how he's by
far the best-looking guy in the band. All to
which I manage to just nod and keep my mouth
shut. Talk about self-control.

It's not that I want to be insincere to Allie, or
Laura for that matter, but I just don't feel it's

right for me to have these feelings for Jeremy. Or
to express them. I don't see that any good could
come from any of it. And although he's never
admitted it, I suspect by a couple of comments
from Isaiah that Jeremy might have a girl back
home. Naturally, I hope I'm wrong. But all these
thoughts about dating and crushes and boys just
leave me feeling a bit empty and weary. In fact, I
don't think it's very healthy for me. So I'll return
to what I should be doing at the moment, and
that's songwriting.

MY HEART'S YOUR HEART

You carved a niche inside of me

a pleasant, quiet space

a room that's fit for a great King

and it's the very place

for You to live and dwell and stay

so that we're not apart

dear God, i want Your home to be

always inside my heart

amen

Thursday, November 11

(SINGING BIG IN ST. LOUIS)

We had one of our best concert crowds last night.
They were absolutely fantastic and I felt like I
could've performed all night. But we politely

surrendered the stage when it was time for Iron Cross to perform. Still, I think the crowd may have liked us almost as much as them. Okay, I know that's a very egotistical thing to say. But the reason has to do with CD sales and comments after the show. For the first time, Redemption outsold Iron Cross after the concert. It was almost embarrassing.

"It was probably just because everyone here already has your CDs," Willy assured the other band members as we all kicked back over a late dinner of pizza afterward.

"Oh, yeah," Jeremy said with a playful roll of his eyes. "That must be it."

"It's just a fluke," I told them as I reached for another slice of triple cheese pizza.

Isaiah laughed. "Pretty nice fluke for Redemption."

"You girls need to accept the fact that you're getting really good," said Jeremy. "The crowd loved you tonight. And that's cool."

Michael nodded. "It took us a couple of years to get the kind of response you're getting on your first tour."

"Well, that's probably because we're opening for you," said Allie.

"Yeah," agreed Laura. "You guys draw the big crowds, and we get to come along for the ride."

"It's a great ride too." I smiled at Jeremy, then

glanced at the others. "Thanks for letting us tag along."

"Yeah, we'll probably be saying the same thing to you someday," said Brett.

I hardly think so. And it's not that I'd want to bump Iron Cross from their nearly constant number one position on the Christian music charts, but I wouldn't mind seeing us at least make an appearance someday. Maybe in the number ten spot. Still, I know that's a long shot this early in the game. Eric said that we don't need to worry about numbers yet. But it's hard not to hope. Just the same, I better put the whole thing back in God's hands.

YOU'RE THE ONE
make us, break us, lift us high
use us, lose us, let us die
You're the one who sets our fate
plans our futures, bad or great
lead us, feed us, show Your way
hold us, mold us, every day
You're the one who knows it all
if we stand or if we fall
boom us, doom us, it's Your choice
teach us, reach us with Your voice
You're the One, the One who must
bring us to this place of trust
amen

Sunday, November 21

(DANCING IN DES MOINES)

We had our final concert last night before our Thanksgiving break. Laura's and my parents drove over to see us perform again. Then after the concert, Laura decided to go home with her parents. I think that was a good choice because it seems as if she's been getting a little tired and strung out again. She's really due for a rest.

I decided to stay on the bus and come home with the rest of the crew. Somehow just knowing I'll be home by tonight is a huge comfort to me. And then I don't have to do anything I don't want to do for four lovely days. But it's back on the road on Friday.

This morning, as we all met for breakfast in the hotel, I asked Jeremy what he was doing for Thanksgiving.

"Our parents have this great big celebration. They have about forty or fifty people there—relatives and friends."

"Yeah," Isaiah chimed in. "When we were little they used to make us get up in front of everyone and sing."

Jeremy laughed. "Stuff yourself on Mom's tough turkey and then watch the Baxter Boys perform. What a day!"

"Sounds like fun to me." Allie glanced over at her mom. "What're we doing this year?"

Elise just shook her head. "I haven't given it much thought."

"Hey, why don't you come over to our house," I suggested, hoping my mom wouldn't mind. "And you too, Willy."

"You sure you aren't sick of us?" asked Willy. "You might want a little break."

"No way. You guys are like family."

"Well, you better check with your real family first, Chloe," said Elise. "They might have other plans."

"Okay, I'll give you guys a call after we get home."

After breakfast I noticed Brett and Allie exchanging phone numbers, and I wondered what was up with that but decided not to ask. As expected, I didn't need to.

"Brett wanted my home phone number," Allie told me as soon as we stepped onto the bus.

"Why?" I asked.

She laughed. "Why not?"

"Allie, you need to leave the poor boy alone," scolded Elise as she got Davie settled with a pile of picture books.

"Hey, it was his idea." Allie sank down into the recliner and sighed. "I don't know if I can survive not seeing him for a whole week."

"It's not even a whole week," I reminded her. "Our next concert is on Saturday."

"It'll feel like a month to me."

I picked up my math book and started working on an overdue assignment.

"That's what you should be doing too, Allie," Elise said. "Look, I don't even have to nag Chloe."

"Yeah, yeah." Allie closed her eyes. "Chloe is so perfect. I'll bet you wish she was your daughter."

Elise just laughed, and I took my homework back to the bedroom to finish before I started working on songs and writing in my diary. So far I've managed to stay pretty caught up on schoolwork. But it's not easy. Elise schedules our "school time" in the mornings, and I try to work on it during our free evenings, but it takes a lot of self-discipline sometimes. Still, I don't want to be behind when we return to school after Christmas. I want to prove that it's possible to do a concert tour and continue my schooling. I just hope I can keep it up.

FOR YOU
make me strong
and help me last
so i'll belong
holding fast
to Your hand
and to Your word
help me stand

undeterred
help me know
what is best
when to grow
when to rest
so that all
who see my face
hear Your call
know Your grace
amen

Fourteen

Tuesday, November 23

(HOME SWEET HOME)

The first day back home I mostly slept. My parents didn't even seem to mind. Then today I took a "mental health" day, at least that's what my dad called it. I think it was more of a spiritual health day. I slept in late then spent the rest of the morning reading the new Bible I got while we were in Dallas. I hate to admit that I'd been neglecting to read the Word as much as I should. Anyway, this is going to change now.

My new Bible is actually only the New Testament, and it's called "The Message" and doesn't have the "red lines" that I read before I was a Christian. But to me, the words are more natural sounding—the way people speak today. I like reading it without getting distracted by language. I guess, being a songwriter and all, I'm sort of word sensitive. I read about half of the gospel of John before I decided I could use some fresh air.

So I got out my old bike and rode up to the cemetery. I just walked around and prayed and enjoyed the silence. I'd almost forgotten what silence sounds like. Oh, there was the sound of the wind in the trees and an occasional passing car, but mostly it was very serene. I'm sure if anyone had seen me walking around, they might've thought I was depressed, but I was just enjoying the peace and quiet.

I was also thinking about something that happened the afternoon we got home. Not such a big deal really, but it got me wondering. I was grabbing a few personal items from the medicine cabinet on the bus, like my favorite toothbrush and a bottle of cologne that I got in Santa Fe, when I accidentally knocked Allie's Ritalin bottle into the sink. I picked it up but was slightly surprised to discover that it was empty. I put it back, but when I caught up with Allie in the church parking lot I said, "Hey, I didn't know you'd been taking your Ritalin again."

She looked at me funny. "What do you mean?"

"You know. Your ADD pills."

She just shook her head. "What are you trying to say, Chloe? You think I need to be taking them?"

"No. That's not what I—"

"Look, I've been trying really hard not to be so hyper. Willy said that I was doing a pretty good job too."

"So you have been taking the pills?"

She frowned. "No. I hate those stupid pills.

What are you talking about?"

"Oh. The prescription bottle just fell into the sink, and it sounded like it was empty. That's all."

She considered this. "I bet Mom dumped them. I'd told her explicitly that I had no intention of taking them. She was probably worried about Davie getting into them. Did you know he ate her chocolate-flavored Exlax once? Talk about a stinky disaster. I was doing laundry all day and you should've—"

"Yuck." I held up my hands to stop her. "That's a whole lot more than I wanted to hear."

"Come on, Allie," called Elise. "Willy said he'd drop us at home."

"Call me," said Allie.

"Yeah." I waved over to where my dad was just getting out of his car. "Can you believe we're home?"

Allie grinned. "It feels pretty good, huh?"

I nodded. "Who'd've thunk? See ya, Al!" I picked up my bag and headed over to my dad.

And then I was so busy talking with him and telling him how I'd invited Allie's family and Willy over for Thanksgiving that I completely forgot about the Ritalin thing. But it's been bugging me a little. Elise might've tossed the pills away out of concern for Davie, but why wouldn't she have thrown out the bottle too? I suppose she could've been saving it to have the prescription refilled, just in case Allie changed her mind. But I must admit that I had noticed how Allie seemed a little calmer during the last half of our trip. I really thought she had been taking the Ritalin, but why would she lie to me?

Okay, here's what I was really wondering about: I've noticed that Laura seems different. She went through her funky period early on in the tour, but then she popped out of it. She really appears to have these highs and lows that seem sort of un-Laura-like to me. She used to be the even keeled one among us. And I've noticed that she can seem sort of jittery before and after our concerts—like she's had too much caffeine, but she doesn't even drink much of anything with caffeine.

And so, in the privacy of my diary, I am wondering if Laura could have possibly taken Allie's Ritalin. The strange thing about Ritalin is that it works to calm a hyper person like Allie down, but it's a stimulant, I think an amphetamine, to a normal person. Even as I write this I'm thinking it's completely ridiculous. Maybe I just need to see it in print to realize how crazy that would be. Laura is the straightest person I've ever known. And she has absolutely no tolerance toward drug users. She's the one who says things like: "They just need to make better choices..." or "They could get clean if they wanted to..." or "If they'd just trust God, they could get over their addictions..."

Now, it's not that I disagree with her exactly, but I've always felt it was more complicated than that. Like I know that my friends Jake and Cesar did some drugs (mostly weed), and it wasn't that easy for them to get free, but in time they did. But Spencer is one of those guys who thinks he can't live without it. In my opinion, he's the kind of kid who might be a real addict. Like my brother Caleb. And like Laura's sister, Christine. Laura doesn't like to talk about Christine. I think it's an embarrassment to the Mitchell family. Not unlike Caleb is with us. Although I don't think he embarrasses me. I mostly just feel sorry for him. But I'm pretty sure Christine embarrasses Laura, and that's why she won't talk about it. But I could be wrong.

Anyway, I'm fairly positive that Laura would never take drugs. Other than the pills to help her sleep. I guess I can't know this for sure. But I do know that I'll be keeping a better eye on her during the next month of touring. I may even ask her about it.

WHO KNOWS
who knows
what goes
'round in the heads of others

some try
to lie
to sisters and to brothers
some please
some tease
paste on their happy faces
some quit
some fit
by squeezing in tight spaces
some fret
regret
a world that's dark as night
God knows
He shows
us how to walk in light
He takes
and makes
a life you understand
trust Him
just Him
reach out and take His hand
cm

Fifteen

Wednesday, November 24

(BACK IN SCHOOL)

Laura and Allie and I went to school today. Just for lunchtime, since we're not in any real classes until January. Although I met with my English Lit teacher to get some clarification on an assignment.

It was pretty cool seeing our friends again. Everyone was hugging and laughing, and I thought that things have sure changed at Harrison High. Or maybe it's just me. But I remember a time—was it only a year ago—that I was the misfit there. And now it's like I'm a celebrity. So weird.

Anyway, as friends were clamoring around us and wanting to hear every detail about our concerts and road trip, I noticed Marty Ruez sitting by herself in a corner of the cafeteria. Now, Marty is the girl who had helped me out of a tough jam during my freshman year. She observed Tiffany Knight and her cohorts picking on me and went to the counselor in my defense (after I whacked Kerry in the nose with my backpack). If it hadn't been for Marty, I might've actually had a criminal record. Well, I excused myself and went over to say hi.

"Hey, Marty," I said as I pulled out a chair. "Mind if I join you?"

She blinked in surprise, then immediately flushed with embarrassment. I know that she's really self-conscious. She's pretty overweight and has been picked on a lot by people like Tiffany Knight, although Tiffany keeps reassuring me that she's changed her ways. But I've never picked on Marty, and I've tried to reach out to her a number of times.

"Sure," she said. "If you really want to."

"So, how's your year going so far?"

She just shrugged. "Okay, I guess."

"You're looking good." Now this was the truth. She had on a red sweatshirt that really made her hair look rich and dark.

She smiled and seemed to relax a bit. "Thanks, Chloe. How's the music business going?"

"Not too bad. We were on the road for about three months doing concerts and stuff."

"Yeah, I missed seeing you around here."

"I kind of missed being here too. I didn't think I'd feel that way."

Marty shook her head. "I sure wouldn't miss it."

I laughed. "That's kind of how I felt before we left. But it's good to be back now."

She sighed. "I wish I could get out of this place."

"Hey, you!"

I looked up to see Cesar approaching our table. "Hey, Cesar!" I stood and grinned at him, surprised at how handsome he looked in his off-white sweatshirt and baggy jeans. "I was wondering where you were."

"How about a hug?" he asked.

"Sure." I hugged him then stepped back. "Is hugging legal in your nondating plan?"

He laughed. "Yeah, as long as it's platonic. Hey, Marty, what's up?"

She just shrugged. "Not much."

"Mind if I join you girls?"

Marty's face brightened. "Pull up a chair."

I turned to Marty. "Have you heard that Cesar has given up dating girls?"

"Coming out of the closet, are you?" she asked without batting an eyelash.

This made Cesar laugh. "No, not exactly."

I reached over and patted his hand. "I'm sorry, Cesar. I probably shouldn't go around telling everyone about your new conviction."

"Oh, it's okay." He looked at Marty. "I gave up dating so that I could focus my energy on God better."

She blinked. "For real?"

"Yep. For real."

"I have another friend who's done the same thing," I told her. "She'd been dating my brother—"

"You mean Caitlin O'Conner?"

"Yeah."

"Oh, I knew that." Marty waved her hand as if it was old news.

"Really?"

"Yeah, I heard about it during my freshman year. She was a senior then."

"So anyway, I kind of understand it." I glanced at Cesar and wondered if I really did. And I can't explain it, but suddenly—now that I was face-to-face with him—I had this longing to be closer. Suddenly I wished we were still going together. Even as I write this, I'm thinking it's crazy, but it's how I felt. Maybe it has to do with forbidden fruit. Someone tells you that you can't have it, and it's all you can think about.

"So, are you doing it too?" asked Marty.

"Doing it?" I peered curiously at her.

"You know, the nondating thing?"

I shrugged. "Well, not really. I mean, it's not as if I'm dating anyone. But I haven't really felt like God was telling me it's something I need to give up. My music keeps me so busy that dating is pretty much a nonissue."

"So then I'm not the only one who's lonely on Fridays." Marty attempted a pitiful-looking smile.

"You're lonely on Fridays?" asked Cesar.

She rolled her eyes at him. "Yeah, what'd you think? That boys were lining up at my door?"

"I've been going to youth group on Fridays," said Cesar. "I'd be glad to take you along, if you'd like."

"Really?" Marty looked slightly skeptical. I suspected that she's been teased about something like this before. I've heard mean stories where popular guys will ask a girl like Marty out, acting all serious and sweet, and then, of course, they never show up. But I knew this wasn't Cesar's style.

"Really."

"Okay," she said. "That'd be cool." Then she glanced at her watch. "Guess I better be going."

"I'll give you a call about Friday."

"Great."

I watched Marty walk away, and I'm sure I saw just the slightest spring in her normally heavy step.

I turned and studied him for a moment. "That was really cool, Cesar."

He smiled at me, and for the second time today I thought I was going to crack—I honestly wanted to get right down on my knees and beg Cesar to reconsider this not-going-out thing. But somehow I managed to maintain my dignity.

"Yeah, I've known Marty since grade school. But I guess I sort of forget that her life might be a little lonely sometimes."

I nodded. "Well, that's great that you're going to take her to youth group."

"So tell me all about your trip, Chloe."

"You have time?"

He shrugged. "I don't think the world will fall apart if I miss economics."

I groaned. "Don't you just hate that class?" Then I told him some of the highlights of our trip. I was careful to play down anything to do with Jeremy Baxter. Not that I have anything to hide, exactly, but I guess I didn't want to give the wrong impression either. We must've talked for forty minutes. It felt just like old times, but I could tell it was probably time for him to be getting back to class.

"I've really missed you, Chloe." Cesar stood and shoved his hands in his pockets.

"Me too." I could feel a small lump growing in my throat as I stood with him. "And I hope you understood about—"

"Hey, it's cool." He cut me off. "And as it turns out, I think you were absolutely right."

"But I still feel really close to you, Cesar."

"I know. I want us to stay that way too. Just without dating."

I nodded. "That makes sense."

"So, let's keep e-mailing and stuff. Okay?"

"Yeah. I love getting your e-mails on the road.

You make me feel like I'm back in school."

He frowned. "And that's a good thing?"

"When you're away from home, it is."

"Well, I better get to class before they put out an APB on me." He glanced at the cafeteria clock. "When do you guys hit the road again?"

"Friday morning."

"So, I probably won't see you again."

"Probably not."

He reached over and gave me another hug. "Take care then."

I nodded. "You too."

As he walked away I wanted to call out, "I love you, Cesar." But wisely, I didn't. Still, as I write this, I'm thinking that maybe Cesar was my real "first" love—with a boy anyway. My most important first love is with God. But now I guess I wonder whether it's really over with Cesar or not. In a way I'm sort of relieved that he's not dating. That way I won't have to worry about some other girl, like Marissa, stealing him away. Earlier today, Marissa asked me why we weren't going together anymore, and I told her that Cesar had "kissed dating good-bye."

"You mean kissed you good-bye," she teased.

I shrugged. "I guess it was mutual."

"So it's open season on Cesar then?" Her green eyes twinkled with mischief.

I just laughed. "Hey, if you really think he'll

compromise his commitment for you, well then, good luck."

But somehow I don't think he will. At least I hope not. It's not that I have anything against Marissa—and sometimes I actually think she's seeking God—but in some ways (like when she shoplifted the thongs in the mall!) she's unpredictable. And I don't think a relationship with her would be very good for Cesar.

Anyway, I figured it was about time for us to clear out of school before the vice principal showed up and attempted to force the three of us to his office for playing hooky. I glanced around the mostly empty cafeteria to spy Laura and Allie sitting at a table with a few kids who didn't appear to be in any hurry to get back to class. I went over to join them, but Laura was already getting up to go.

"See ya around," she called over her shoulder to the kids at the table.

"How'd it go with Cesar?" Allie asked as we walked out of the cafeteria.

"Okay. He's really committed to this nondating thing."

"That's so weird," said Allie. "I mean, I kind of understood it when Caitlin shared with our youth group last summer, like from a girl's perspective. But I just don't get a guy doing it."

"What do you mean? Do you have some kind of

double standard for guys? Like it's okay for them to do whatever they want, but girls better watch out?"

"Huh?" Allie seemed to consider this. "Now that you mention it, I suppose that could be true. I mean, we girls just kind of expect guys to act like jerks most of the time, don't we?"

"I don't," snapped Laura. She was unlocking her car now, fumbling to get the key into the lock. "I think guys should be held to the same standard as girls."

"That's easy for you to say. Ryan was a real gentleman," Allie reminded her. "I'm sure he never would've pulled anything stupid."

Laura pressed her lips together as she placed her hands on the steering wheel. "Yeah, probably not. Not that it matters now, but I think I can see why Cesar has given up dating. In fact, I think it might be a good idea for everyone."

"Seriously?" I asked.

"Yes. I think we should all consider it." She turned and looked at us. "I know that you both believe you're in love with—well, I won't mention names—but they happen to belong to a certain Christian rock band that's fairly well known."

"Both of us?" Allie turned and stared at me. "I mean, I've made no secret that I'm a little smitten by a certain Brett James, but what's up with you, Chloe?"

"Wake up and smell the coffee," Laura said in a sharp tone. "It's obvious that Chloe's head over heels in love with Jeremy."

"Jeremy?" Allie sounded truly shocked now. "No way. Chloe is NOT in love with Jeremy. Are you, Chloe?"

Okay, I must confess that I lied at that point. "No," I said quickly, glancing away. "Laura probably just assumed that since Jeremy and I are good friends I must be in love."

Laura narrowed her eyes at me. "So you're saying you're not?"

"That's what I'm saying, Laura. Jeremy and I are just good friends who happen to enjoy spending time together. We talk about music and God and whatever. Besides, what difference does this make to you all of a sudden? And why are you so grumped out today? Get up on the wrong side of bed this morning, did we?"

Laura made a growling sound, then sighed and shook her head. "Oh, I'm sorry. I don't even know why I said that. Maybe I just felt left out."

"Left out?" Allie reached over from the backseat and patted Laura on the shoulder. "You can never be left out, Laura. You know how much we love you. We wouldn't have Redemption without you. Don't you know that by now?"

"Yeah," I chimed in. I sensed that something deeper was bugging Laura. "We're in this thing

together. For better or for worse, you know. Don't
go saying you feel left out."

Then Laura started to cry. She put her head
down on the steering wheel and quietly sobbed. I
didn't know what to say.

"Do you want us to pray for you?" asked Allie
in a quiet voice.

Laura just nodded without speaking.

So there in Harrison High School's visitors'
parking lot, Allie and I prayed for Laura. We
weren't too sure what exactly we were praying for,
but we asked God to comfort her and strengthen
her and to hold her in the palm of His hand. And
when we finished she seemed a little better.

"Thanks, guys." Laura wiped her nose on a tissue, then started the engine and backed up. "I
think the concert tour sort of wiped me out. I
haven't done much of anything besides sleep
since I've been home. I probably shouldn't have
come to visit at school today. But I just wanted to
see my old friends."

"It was cool seeing everyone," I said, "but I
think it was kind of stressful too."

Laura nodded. "It's different than when we're
signing autographs and making small talk with
strangers. That's a lot easier."

I wasn't so sure about that, but I didn't say so.

"Yeah," agreed Allie. "I hope that life will
feel more normal when we come back to school

after Christmas break. Today was kind of weird."

"Keep getting rested up," I told Laura as she dropped me at home.

"I will."

Still, I feel a little worried about Laura. It's weird too, because of the three of us, I would think that Allie or I would be the ones to have problems just based on our personality types—Allie being the hyper one and me being the more melancholy. Anyway, you'd think that Laura would have it all together by now.

I'm really going to be praying for Laura. I guess I'm afraid that she's having second thoughts about the band. I'm worried that she might decide not to go back on the road with us. And where would that leave us? Nowhere, I'm afraid.

HANG ON TO HER
hanging by a thread
or so it seems
in a moment, dashed,
are all our dreams
life can take a turn
and then a swerve
spinning in a circle
around a curve
hanging to the rope
she fights for life

shouting to be heard
above the strife
hold on, dear God, please
don't let her go
hanging on to her
just let her know
that she can relax
and lean on You
You're the only One
to get her through
carry her along
don't let her fall
not until she's given
You her all
amen

Sixteen

Friday, November 26

(ON THE ROAD AGAIN)

I must admit that it feels kind of good to be back on tour. And to my great relief, Laura is here with us and pretty much acting like everything is okay. Although she does seem a bit different to me. A little closed off, like she's keeping to herself more. But maybe she just needs that kind of space. In a way, I suppose I do too. Sometimes all this 24/7 closeness and interaction takes its toll on me.

According to the schedule that Willy just posted on our bus bulletin board, we have eight concerts to do before Christmas. All of them are in the northeast, and he told us to pray for good weather.

I had a nice Thanksgiving with my family. Naturally, Josh was home and my grandparents came. In fact, my grandma did most of the cooking, although I did help her make pumpkin and pecan pies, which weren't half bad if I do say so. My parents said it was okay to invite Allie's family as well as Willy. And I think they were glad to join us. All in all, it was a pretty low-key event but exactly what I needed after the fast-paced stress of the last few weeks of our concert tour.

Caitlin and her brother, Benjamin, came over in the evening, and we played some board games and just visited for a while. I can't believe how much older Ben seems now. He's in the same grade as I am, but I've always thought of him as younger. Actually, he is younger since I'm old in my class. But he really seems to have grown up a lot since last spring.

I still think that Caitlin and Josh will get married someday. You can just tell by the way they interact and look at each other. There is definitely something going on. But they keep saying they're only friends. And hey, that's cool. When the time's right, we'll all be happy for them.

Speaking of couples, I think that Willy likes Elise. It's not that he does anything overt, but he is very respectful of her and treats her like she's special. I know she enjoys that too, especially considering the way Allie's father had treated her in the past. It's kind of fun to watch. I'm not sure if Allie has noticed it yet or not, or even what she'd think if something were to develop. But I could imagine those two together. And little Davie just adores Willy. I'm sure he'd welcome him as a new "daddy." Still, I don't think I'll say anything to anyone. No use rushing things.

Speaking of rushes, I am really looking forward to seeing Jeremy again. But more than ever now, I know I'll have to be very careful not to show my feelings. I feel bad that I lied to Laura and Allie, and yet I'm not sure how I could've handled it better. I don't think it would do anyone a bit of good to know that I've got a thing for Jeremy Baxter. Besides, it's probably just one of those schoolgirl crushes that should go away in time. Sigh...

Mostly, I need to stay focused on my music and songwriting and, of course and foremost, God. That's enough to keep me busy—and out of trouble.

DEEPER FOR YOU
like a tree that's growing strong
branches reaching, stretching long
toward the warmth of sweet sunshine
tall and healthy, green and fine
without roots my tree would tumble
it would topple down and crumble
it's my roots that hold me fast
digging deep so i can last
through the storms and winds that blow
it's my roots that hold me so
and it's the roots that feed my tree
digging deep so i can be
hale and hearty, strong and tall
deeply rooted, i won't fall

cm

Sunday, November 28

(FLAT IN INDIANAPOLIS)

Redemption's portion of last night's concert felt
a little flat to me, not musically speaking since
I'm sure we were on key, but something about it
felt slightly off. As usual, we prayed before the
concert. And the audience responded positively.
If they noticed anything amiss, they sure didn't
show it.

Allie gave a brief testimony afterward, sharing about how she once believed that Wicca was
the answer for her, but she was only disappointed
by it in the end, and the crowd appeared to be gen-
uinely moved. But the concert, or our part in it,
still felt less than great to me.

Jeremy spied me looking a little glum after we
finished signing CDs and asked what was wrong.

"I don't know." I shook my head. "But I just
don't think we were very good tonight."

"We as in everyone?"

"No," I assured him. "I mean we as in
Redemption. I don't think we played as well as we
should."

"You girls sounded great."

But I think he was just trying to be nice. I
think we sounded blah, dull, flat. In my mind,
something was definitely missing. I just couldn't
put my finger on what.

"Sometimes it's hard to get back into the

groove after being home for a few days," he told me as we gathered our stuff backstage.

"It didn't sound like you guys were having any problem," I said.

Michael laughed. "Hey, it didn't sound like you girls were having any problem either. Don't be so tough on yourself, Chloe."

Jeremy patted me on the back. "It's okay. I know exactly how you feel. These guys are always telling me that I'm our worst critic."

"You and Chloe," added Allie. "She's always harping at us to try harder, play better. Sometimes I think she should carry a whip."

Jeremy grinned. "It's just the way we're wired. Right, Chloe?"

I nodded. "Yeah, blame it on God."

And I didn't mean that in a bad way. I only meant that God really has made us all differently. And that's cool. It'd be pretty boring if we were all alike. And I'm sure our music would sound awful.

BLAME IT ON GOD
none of us are the same
guess it's God who gets the blame
creatively, He made each one
no two alike beneath the sun
all our gifts are different
each of them is heaven sent

and yet He fits us all together
so we'll glorify Him forever
cm

Monday, December 6

(THE PITS IN PITTSBURGH)

Something is wrong with Laura. I can feel it in my bones. But no one else seems to be noticing. So today I decided to ask her what's up. We're staying at a hotel until our concert on Wednesday. So after practice today, since Allie had promised to watch Davie while Elise went to get a haircut, I invited Laura to get some lunch with me. We made sure we had a good supply of Mickey D-bucks in our pockets since I felt fairly certain we'd get sp'anged within a few feet of the hotel. And we did. Laura got to do the giving, but I got to tell the girl that Jesus loved her and had a better plan for her life.

We decided to go to a sushi bar. Thanks to the influence of Iron Cross, all three of us have acquired a taste for sushi lately. And believe me, it's an acquired taste. It took Allie three times before she could eat raw fish without gagging. Now she acts as if she's been eating sushi since infancy.

After we finished our food, I requested a refill on my iced tea and then asked Laura how she was feeling.

"Huh?" She looked at me funny. "What do you mean?"

I stirred the ice with my straw. "I mean, how are you feeling? Everything okay?"

She frowned. "Yeah. Why?"

"I don't know, Laura. You just seem different."

"Different, like how?"

I took a deep breath and prayed a silent prayer. I wasn't quite sure how to say what I wanted to say. "Well, you seem more moody than you used to be."

She shrugged. "Like Willy says, touring can bring out the worst in people."

I nodded. "I know. It's not easy for any of us."

"It seems to be easy for you and Allie. You guys always appear to be on top of things. Looks like I'm the one who's always messing stuff up."

"You don't mess stuff up."

"Then why are you sitting here telling me I'm moody?"

"Because I think something is wrong, Laura."

Now she looked directly at me. "What do you think is wrong?"

"Honestly?"

"Yeah, honestly. What do you think is wrong, Chloe?"

"Okay, I know this might sound silly. But I've wondered if you might be, uh, well..." Suddenly I didn't think I could say the words aloud. I mean, it would sound perfectly ridiculous.

"What?" she demanded.

I sighed deeply. "Okay, let me explain something."

"Fine," she said with obvious exasperation. "Go ahead and explain."

"Well, right before Thanksgiving, after we got home, I accidentally knocked Allie's prescription bottle, the one for her Ritalin, out of the medicine cabinet in the bus." I paused to study Laura's reaction, and I'm certain I saw a flash of something in her eyes. Was it fear or simply indignation? I'm still not entirely sure.

"Anyway," I continued. "I noticed the bottle was empty, and I just figured that Allie had been taking her Ritalin pills again."

Laura had a blank expression now, as if she'd pulled a curtain over her face. "And?"

"But Allie said she hadn't."

"So?"

"So, I thought it was odd that the bottle was empty."

"What are you saying, Chloe? Are you accusing me of taking Allie's Ritalin pills?"

"Nooo." I looked out the window, suddenly wishing I'd never brought this up. "But it occurred to me that you've been acting differently. You don't seem like you used to be."

"Hey, we've all changed. You can't do something like this concert tour without changing, Chloe."

"Yeah, I know. But you seem more changed than anyone, Laura. And I just thought it was possible that—"

"That I've become a drug addict? That I would steal Allie's pills?" She stood up now and fumbled to find money for the bill. "I can't believe you. I thought you were my friend."

"I am your friend. That's why I'm having this conversation with you." I set a ten on the table and followed Laura to the exit.

She paused with her hand on the door, then turned to me with a hurt expression. "You know how I feel about drugs."

"I know; I know."

"Then why are you doing this to me?"

"I'm just worried about you."

"Am I messing up when we perform?"

"No."

"Am I falling apart?"

I shook my head.

"Then why?"

I put my hand on her shoulder. "Look, I'm sorry, Laura. I know it was stupid of me to think that. But you know what happened to my brother, and even your sister. I know that drugs are real and they can really mess you up." I noticed a group of kids hanging on the corner across the street. I don't like to judge, but just the way they were huddled together, looking sort of down and out and basically burnt, just seemed to suggest drugs. "Look at those guys over there."

She glanced across the street, then turned back to me with a sour scowl. "Are you suggesting that I'm like them?"

"No, that's not what I mean. I'm just saying that it can happen to anyone. I'm guessing every one of those kids used to be a normal kid like us, like my brother Caleb and your sister. But I'm guessing that somewhere along the line they might've got hooked on dope. And now it's probably destroying their whole lives."

"What makes you such an expert, Chloe?"

"I'm not. But I guess I'm trying to understand it better, and Willy has explained some things..." But I quit talking when I realized she was tuning me out.

Laura had already started walking back toward the hotel. "You can believe whatever you want," she called over her shoulder. "But I am not like them. I am not an addict. And I am hurt that you would think that of me."

I hurried to catch her and apologized all the way back to the hotel. By the time we reached the lobby, I felt lower than the snuffed-out cigarette butt that the doorman was removing from the entryway carpet.

"Fine. I'll forgive you, Chloe." Laura pushed the floor number in the elevator without looking at me. "As long as you never bring this up again."

I looked down at the floor. "Believe me, I won't."

So now I not only feel like a total jerk but a complete fool as well. I can't believe that I actually thought I was doing the right thing to ask her about this. And maybe I was, since the Bible tells us to go directly to anyone we have a problem with. Pastor Tony has taught this numerous times. But somehow it just didn't work today.

THE RIGHT THING
what first seemed right
just turned out wrong
the road seemed short
but now it's long
what started good
quickly turned bad
became a mess
and now she's mad
when will i learn
to hold my peace
to wait on God
for His release
when will i see
my right is wrong
i need God's help

to get along
i think i'm big
then see i'm small
to You, my Lord,
i give it all
cm

Seventeen

Sunday, December 12
(BUFFALO BLAHS)

Okay, even Willy said he thinks something was missing in our performance last night. I know I was feeling down and consequently not playing my best. It's like there's a wall between Laura and me now. And Allie is sort of stuck in the middle, so I'm sure she's not doing her best either. Fortunately, the crowd didn't seem to notice anything. But then they've never heard us when we're really hot. Besides, Iron Cross is supposed to be the star of the show. Believe me, they were last night. A huge relief. I almost think they do better when we play badly, but that could just be me.

Anyway, after Willy took us to church this morning, he asked if he could have a meeting after our practice this afternoon. I should mention that we don't usually practice on Sundays since it's supposed to be our day of rest. But sometimes, like if we've played badly or have a big concert coming up, we go ahead and practice and try to make sure we have some downtime later.

So after practice, Willy set some bags of chips

and some cans of sodas on the table in the practice room. "So how do you girls think you sounded last night?"

I just groaned and grabbed a soda.

"Pretty cruddy," said Allie.

Laura didn't say anything.

"I don't like to criticize, but it feels as though something isn't working," he continued as he pulled up a chair. "Like something is missing." His eyes moved over the three of us, as if looking for clues.

"Well, I agree," I said. "Something is definitely missing."

"What is it?" He leaned back in his chair and waited for someone to respond, but no one did.

"Are you girls getting along all right?" he finally asked.

"I don't know..." I glanced over at Laura who seemed to be having a silent vigil.

"It's been kinda different lately." Allie looked at me and then Laura. "I think something's bugging those two."

Willy nodded. "You wanna talk about it?"

"Yeah," I said. "I'm sure not enjoying the way things are going right now."

"How about you, Laura?" he asked. "Willing to talk?"

She shrugged. "I guess."

I decided to lay my cards on the table. "First of

all," I began slowly. "I guess I should say that this is probably all my fault." Although, to be perfectly honest, I'm not entirely sure that's completely true. Still, it seemed a good place for me to start. And hopefully it would put Laura at ease.

"How's that?" asked Willy.

"Well, I sort of hurt Laura's feelings last week. I told her I was sorry and everything, but I think she might still be feeling bad about it." I said this without looking at Laura.

"What'd you do?" asked Allie with her typical wide-eyed curiosity, which some might mistake for nosiness. But when you know Allie, you can be fairly certain that it's really just concern.

I glanced at Laura, and she was doing her stone impression again. Just staring at the chips and sodas splayed across the table as if they were really fascinating.

I took in a deep breath, unsure of how much I should say. "I made sort of an accusation." I could tell by the sharp glint in Laura's eyes that she didn't want to go there.

"What kind of accusation?" asked Willy. Then he cleared his throat. "The only reason I'm asking is because you girls are like a family, and there's no point in keeping secrets from anyone. We need to get stuff out into the open, you know what I mean?"

I nodded. "I guess so. I just don't want to make

Laura feel bad all over again."

Willy turned to Laura. "Are you okay with this?"

She just rolled her eyes. "Whatever."

So I repeated pretty much what I'd said to Laura about how she seemed different and how Allie's Ritalin pills were gone.

"Oh, yeah," said Allie. "I remember you mentioned that at Thanksgiving. I meant to ask Mom about it, but everything got so busy."

"So you didn't take the pills, Allie?" Willy asked.

"No, I've told you how much I hate taking them. And I thought I'd been doing better at keeping myself calm." She frowned. "Don't you think I've been doing better?"

Willy laughed. "Yeah, mostly."

"Anyway, I told Chloe that my mom probably just threw them out."

"Did you ask your mom?" I asked.

"No. But she and Davie are probably still upstairs. I could call and ask her now," suggested Allie. "Would that help clear things up?"

Laura folded her arms across her chest. "You might as well call her if we're going to finish up our little Spanish Inquisition."

"Is that how you really feel, Laura?" asked Willy. "I only want to help you girls clear this up—whatever it is."

"Fine," Laura sighed in exasperation. And I

could feel myself squirming in my chair. Why hadn't I just kept my big mouth shut?

But Allie was already on the phone. We could hear her asking Elise the question, followed by a long pause as she listened to the response.

"Thanks, Mom." Then she hung up and turned back to face us. "Uh, my mom said she didn't do any-thing with my pills. In fact, she actually thought that I'd been taking them." Allie sort of smiled. "I guess that's kind of a compliment to me."

"But not to me." Laura stood now. "I suppose you all think I'm some sort of drug addict because Allie's stupid pills are missing. So just like that I'm charged as guilty. Right?"

"We're not saying that," Willy said in a calm voice. "But stranger things have been known to happen on concert tours."

Laura was pacing now. "Well, it just figures. You guys have ganged up on me before. I'm used to being the minority—"

"What?" I said. "When have we ever ganged up—?"

"You and Allie!" She pointed her finger at us. "You two are always pairing up, and then I get pushed out—"

"Just a minute," I said. "If anyone's been pushed aside lately, it's been me."

"Or me," said Allie. "You and Laura went to lunch the other day and left me behind, and you guys always—"

"Hold on." Willy held up his hands. "I think we're getting off track here."

Laura stopped pacing and just stared at us. "I think you're all against me."

"No one's against anyone," said Willy. "We're just trying to figure out what's wrong here because something is very definitely wrong."

"And everyone's pointing the finger at me." Laura had tears in her eyes now.

"Not really, Laura," I said. "I actually started this whole thing by saying that I thought I may be the one to blame. I never should've made that accusation. And I told you then that I was sorry. And I'm still sorry."

Laura was crying now. I went over and put my arm around her shoulders. "I wouldn't have said anything except that you seem so different to me. You used to be like the Rock of Gibraltar. Sometimes Allie or I could be a little flaky, but we could always count on you to be the even-keeled one. But it seems as though you've been moodier than ever. And when I saw those pills missing, well, I just wondered..."

"It's a fairly natural conclusion," said Willy.

"Thanks a lot!" snapped Laura.

"Although that doesn't make it true," he continued without even reacting to her barb. I really admire how Willy can keep his cool in every situation. It's a good quality for a manager. "It's only circumstantial evidence, Laura."

"So I AM on trial!"

"No one is on trial here." Willy stood and went over to where Laura and I were already standing. "I think we need to pray."

Then Allie joined us, and the three of us surrounded Laura as Willy led a prayer. "Dear Heavenly Father," he prayed. "Please, bring Your truth to light. Heal our broken relationships and comfort our hearts as only You can. And finally, we ask that You would bind us together in Your gracious love."

Then we all said, "Amen."

"I told my mom I'd call her this afternoon." Laura wiped her nose. "Are we done here?"

"I guess so," said Willy. But I could tell by his expression that he was still concerned.

After Laura left, I asked Willy if he thought I'd been wrong to confront Laura last week.

"That's between you and God, Chloe."

"I know. But what do you really think? Would you have done it?"

He slowly nodded. "Under the circumstances and knowing the pressure that you girls are under, I'm sure I would've."

"Do you think Laura has actually been taking my Ritalin?"

"It's possible, Allie," said Willy. "And in Laura's defense, you need to understand that these things can and do happen. We all know she's had a really hard time on this trip. First it was the sleeping problem, and then she couldn't get herself going..." He sighed and shook his head. "I think there's a possibility that Chloe is right on."

Allie looked troubled. "But what do we do now?"

"There's not much we can do unless Laura actually admits to it. There's always the chance that we're all wrong. She may be telling the truth. For her sake I hope so."

"But where did the Ritalin go?"

Willy studied us both then grinned. "Who knows? Maybe I took it. Or Rosy. Or Elise."

"Yeah, sure," said Allie. "And maybe Davie took it, and that's why he's so wired. Although they might not work like that on him since he doesn't have ADD. It's funny how that drug works one way on one person and completely the opposite on the other."

Willy went over to the table and started cleaning up our snack mess. "I've heard the street value on uppers like that could be up to thirty dollars a pop."

"Wow, good thing I didn't know that back during my godless, rebellious period," Allie said as she threw the empty soda cans in the trash. "I might've become a drug dealer."

"Yeah, I can just see you pushing pills back in middle school," I teased.

"Hey, we all know it happens."

"But getting back to the problem," I said. "What should we do now?"

"Well, until we can figure this out, I'd suggest you girls keep a close eye on Laura without her feeling as if she's being spied on. And try not to treat her differently. She's already feeling very sensitive, and the last thing she needs is to feel like we're all against her. Because we're not. She needs to know that we love her regardless of anything that may or may not be going on."

"Unconditionally," said Allie.

"That's right," I added. "The same way God loves us."

It's not much of a plan, but for the time being it's all we have. Well, that and a lot of prayer. Once again it feels as if Redemption hangs in the balance. Will we ever get beyond these challenges, or will our band simply become obsolete before we have a chance to really make it big? To be perfectly honest, it makes me mad. Not at Laura exactly, because if she's really using drugs, I know she must be feeling totally horrible. Maybe I'm mad at Satan, because I know, according to God's Word, that he wants to destroy us. And I'm sure drugs could do that. So I'll set my heart to continue loving Laura despite all this and trust God with the rest.

DESPITE IT ALL
we blow it
once again
same mistake
same old sin
you would think
we would learn
to avoid
the same old burn
but we trip
then we fall
on our face
before all
with eyes shut
how we stumble
foot in mouth
how we bumble
despite all
Jesus lives
takes our hands
and forgives
picks us up
makes us new
loves despite
the things we do
cm

Eighteen

Wednesday, December 15

(BROKEN IN BALTIMORE)

I feel as if I've been walking on eggshells the past couple days—trying to love Laura, attempting to encourage her, and yet constantly offending her. Or so it seems. I don't understand why she's so defensive. Doesn't she know how much we love her? Yet no matter what I say, she seems to take it the wrong way. I complimented her on her outfit yesterday, and she went and changed her clothes!

She also seems very secretive, or maybe she just wants her privacy, which I can sort of understand because I'm a fairly private person myself. But the last few days she's either locked in the bedroom in the back of the bus, or on her cell phone, or just plain checked out behind a book. And this makes it difficult to "keep an eye on her" like Willy suggested. Worse than that, it seems to confirm my suspicions. I feel fairly certain that she's using something.

Now I must say that it still seems very weird to think this about her. After all, Laura is the last person on the planet you would ever suspect to have a drug problem. She never liked being around the kids who were known to use either drugs or alcohol. In fact, she didn't even like to be around anyone who smoked. Laura used to be a real zero-tolerance kind of girl. I wish that were still true, but deep in my gut I really believe she's using.

However, I've decided not to discuss this with anyone for the time being. Not until we know something for sure. I'm hoping that Willy and Allie will come to their own conclusions. Also, Elise and Rosy have been informed that we might have trouble.

I think I've gotten over feeling mad about this whole nasty business, and the fact that Laura might have a drug problem doesn't make me love her any less. If anything, I think I love her more because I can see how vulnerable she is right now. Not that I approve of drugs. I certainly do NOT. I've seen way too many lives wrecked because of drugs. Including my brother Caleb's.

But it still bugs me that Laura won't come clean and admit that something's up. Of course, at the same time, this also makes me question myself. I've actually wondered whether I had just imagined the whole thing. Like maybe Laura was getting framed for something she hadn't even done. Crud, I'm sure that alone could make you act pretty weird. But something happened tonight that makes me believe I must be right.

We were in the middle of our performance in Baltimore when Laura started falling apart. First she was just missing it on bass and fading out on vocals. But then she quit playing altogether in the middle of our "Safety Zone" song—which really needs a strong bass, not to mention her voice, to make it sound good. Anyway, Allie and I managed to finish up the song, but I know it must've sounded pretty lame.

Then I turned around to look at Laura, and she was standing there with tears streaming down her face. So, feeling rattled and nervous, I started talking to the audience. Thinking I'd buy her some time to get herself back together, I tried to use this moment to connect with the crowd. Besides, I reminded myself, it's not that odd to take a little break to talk to the audience in the middle of a concert. Cool things can happen when we do that.

"You know, I need to remind you that we're real people," I told them. "Sometimes when you're just jiving at a concert, you forget that the bands onstage are made up of living, breathing people. We can get tired or bummed or even constipated occasionally." This brought a few good laughs. "But I guarantee you that we are very real. And like you guys, we have very real problems."

About this time Michael came onto the stage

and started whispering something to Laura. He
already had his bass strapped on, and I could
tell he was offering to step in for her.

"And tonight our bass player, Laura Mitchell,
is having a really tough time. But normally she
is the hottest bass player around..." Then I nodded in Michael's direction. "Well, other than
Michael White from Iron Cross, that is." At the
sound of that name the crowd burst into cheers
and applause, Michael took a cheesy little bow,
and Laura slipped backstage.

"You gonna join us girls tonight, Michael?" I
asked.

He grinned. "If you'll have me."

I turned to the crowd. "What do you think?
Will we have Michael White, the bass player from
Iron Cross?"

Naturally they all cheered wildly, and we
began to play again. I realized that Michael
didn't know all our songs, but he's such a great
bass player that he just jumped right in and
really jammed with us. Of course, he didn't know
the lyrics, but he did a good job adding his own
creative bits of harmony, and I don't think we
sounded too bad. What could've been a total
disaster actually turned into a pretty cool performance. Thank God!

Laura had already returned to the hotel by
the time we finished up. Willy put her in a cab,

then called Elise and instructed her to meet Laura in the lobby.

"What're we gonna do now?" Allie asked as the three of us huddled backstage.

"Should we end the tour?" I spoke the words I hated to hear.

"I don't know." Willy sighed and shook his head. "Maybe so. It looks like Laura is falling apart on us."

"I wish she'd tell us what's going on," I said. "I don't even care if it is drugs. I just want her to be honest about it."

Willy rubbed his chin. "We may need to confront her. Not tonight though. I have a feeling she'll be too wiped out to talk. We'll have a meeting of the minds in the morning."

"Do you need to let Omega know?" I asked weakly. "Will they cancel our contract now?"

"I'm not sure what our next step should be. Let's all pray about it, and then tomorrow we'll do what needs to be done. We still don't know for sure that Laura's using anything. She may just be stressed out."

"Do you really believe that?" asked Allie.

He looked at the floor. "No, not really."

And so I've been praying for Laura all night. Willy was right; she had crashed by the time we got back to the hotel. I'm sure she didn't want to see any of us.

TRUTH HURTS
sometime it's hard
to face the facts
to tell the truth
to feel the ax
sometimes it's tough
to own your mess
to say i failed
to just confess
the truth can hurt
you'll feel the pain
but when it's done
you'll see the gain
you'll see the load's
been taken 'way
and you can face
another day
so though it hurts
momentarily
embrace the Truth
and be set free!
cm

Friday, December 17

(BOSTON BLUES)

We confronted Laura yesterday morning. We knew
we had a full day of travel ahead of us, and Willy
suggested we just get it over with right after we

finished breakfast in the hotel restaurant.

I have to say that I've never seen Laura looking so blue before. It's as if her face were hanging clear down to her knees. She hadn't said a single word and barely touched her food. I really felt sorry for her, but I think we handled it just right.

"We need to pray," announced Willy after Elise and Davie excused themselves to see that our stuff was getting loaded onto the bus. Rosy remained at the table with us. She's been a solid support to Laura through this whole ordeal. She told me that she had an aunt who got hooked on heroine at a young age and died of an overdose while still in her twenties. She understands this stuff.

Willy began to pray. "Dear God, please open our hearts right now and let us speak with honesty and love. We invite Your presence and ask You to guide us through what could be a difficult conversation. In Jesus' name we pray. Amen."

Laura's head remained bowed as Willy cleared his throat and started to speak. "Laura, we are all very concerned for you."

She continued looking down at her plate, and the rest of us just waited for Willy to continue.

"We know you're having a struggle, and it looks like you are losing. We love you like a sister, and when you're hurting, we are all hurting.

We just want to do whatever it takes to get you through this."

Laura slowly lifted her head to reveal two streams of tears streaking her bronzed cheeks. Her eyes looked tired and sad, and her chin was quivering. "I-I'm sorry," she managed to sputter.

Rosy handed her a tissue and put her hand on Laura's shoulder. "It's okay, baby. Go ahead and get it out."

Laura sniffed and wiped her nose, then looked around the table. "I don't know how to say this—" She started to cry again.

"We love you, Laura," I placed my hand on her arm. "You know we love you. We don't care what's wrong; we'll still love you. If we stick together, I think we can get through this."

"That's right," said Willy. "But you've got to be honest with us."

"Come on, Laura," urged Allie. "There's nothing you can tell us that we probably don't already know. You just need to get it out into the open."

"Okay." Laura held her chin up. "You guys were right. I did take Allie's Ritalin." Then she looked back down as if she was horribly embarrassed.

I gently squeezed her arm. "It's okay, Laura. We still love you. You gotta know that. We realized you were having a hard time."

"Yeah," said Allie. "Why don't you just tell us what happened. Get it all out."

Laura looked back up and nodded. "You're right. It's just hard to say. I'm so ashamed."

"Hey," said Willy. "You're a really strong Christian, Laura, but you're only human. God knows we're going to make mistakes. It's how we handle the aftermath that makes all the difference."

"Yeah, I can believe that about other people. It's just hard to believe it about myself. I feel so rotten and hopeless and stupid. I'm such a fool."

"God can work all things together for your good, Laura," I loosely quoted one of my favorite Bible verses. "When you love Him and obey Him. And despite what's happened, we all know that you want to do that."

"I do. I just can't believe I've blown it so bad. It probably started with those stupid sleeping pills." She shook her head. "They did help me sleep, but they made me feel so groggy and dull the following day. It's like I just couldn't get going. And remember how Eric almost didn't let us open for Iron Cross that first time, back in LA? Well, I knew it would be completely my fault if Redemption failed. And I knew I needed something to get me going that night, especially after I'd promised everyone that I could get it together in time for our performance."

"And you did get it together," said Allie. "You were fantastic."

"It was the Ritalin," Laura admitted in a flat voice. "I'd gone down to the bus the day before to get a pair of shoes. And while I was down there, I remembered Allie's pills in the medicine cabinet. I knew that they were actually some kind of pep pill for people who don't have ADD, and I wondered if they would help me get out of that funk that the sleeping pills brought on. So I sneaked a pill out of the bottle and saved it for the next night—for our first opening performance."

"That's why you were so great that night," I said.

She nodded sadly. "At first I was only taking them for concert nights, but then it got so I could hardly function without them. I told myself that a doctor would probably prescribe them for me if I'd had time to go in for an appointment." She sighed. "But I knew deep down that wasn't true. And I always knew it was wrong. The guilt feels like I'm wearing a coat made of lead."

"But what did you do when you ran out of pills?" asked Allie. "My mom said it was only a month's supply."

"I begged my parents to invite my sister to come over for Thanksgiving."

"Christine?" I asked, knowing full well that Christine has a serious drug problem.

"Yeah. They let me call her, and I asked her for pills. She came for Thanksgiving, and I paid three hundred dollars for enough to get me to the end of the tour."

"Three hundred dollars!" Allie just shook her head.

"At the time it didn't seem so bad." Laura looked back down at her plate. "But I know it was wrong and stupid and sinful."

"So where do you go from here, Laura?" asked Willy in a kind voice.

She looked up. "What do you mean?"

"I mean with the drugs."

"Oh." Her eyes darted from face to face. "Well, I've quit taking them, if that's what you mean."

"When?" he asked. "When did you stop?"

"The day you guys asked me about it in the practice room. I decided then and there that I had to stop. I knew it was way out of hand."

"How long ago was that?" asked Rosy.

Laura held up five fingers.

"And how you been doing, baby?" Rosy's voice was full of compassion.

Laura frowned. "Not so great. I'm sure you've all noticed. That's why I fell apart at the concert last night. That's how useless I am without the pills." Her eyes filled with tears again. "I guess I've ruined it for everyone now. I'm sure we'll get canceled."

No one said anything, but I suspect we all agreed with her. There's no way Omega would let us continue to open for Iron Cross. For one thing, we sound horrible with Laura in this condition. But more important, you can't very well have an' addict performing at Christian concerts.

"What about tomorrow night's concert?" asked Allie. "Can Omega find a new warm-up band by then?"

"I seriously doubt it," said Willy.

"Do you think there's any way you could pull it together for just one more night?" I pleaded with Laura, then I stopped myself. "I'm sorry. I guess that's pretty selfish on my part."

"Actually, I think I'm the one who's been pretty selfish," she admitted. "I mean, I really thought I was doing it for the band to start with. But when I continued taking the pills, I knew it was because I liked the feeling I got when I was high. I suppose I truly am an addict."

"Anyone can become an addict," said Rosy. "All you have to do is give in to whatever wrong urge comes along. You do it for long enough and— presto!—you become an addict."

"I knew I was playing with fire," Laura continued. "I knew that every single one of us could get burned because of me. Oh, I'm really, really sorry, you guys! I know you'll forgive me, but I wouldn't blame you if you didn't. You have every right to be totally furious with me. I'm so sorry."

We all reassured her that we forgive her and

love her and are glad that she finally told us the truth.

"But what about tomorrow's concert?" persisted Allie. "We can't just leave Iron Cross high and dry."

Laura nodded. "You're right, Al. We can't do that to them. Especially when I think of how Michael stepped in to help me last night. Somehow I've got to pull myself together for them."

"Is that even possible?" I asked.

"All things are possible with God." Suddenly her chin grew firm, and I thought I saw a spark of confidence from the old Laura. "Okay, I know I could be totally wrong, but somehow I think that I might be able to do this."

"The last time you said that was when you started taking my Ritalin," Allie reminded her.

"I know. But that won't be the case now."

"Do you still have the pills your sister sold you?" asked Rosy.

"I flushed them down the toilet five days ago. I was afraid not to."

"Good girl." Rosy patted her on the back. "You know the difference between a fool and righteous man, baby?"

Laura shook her head.

"Well, a fool falls down once and just stays down. Whereas a righteous man might fall down a lot, but every single time he gets right back up."

"With the help of God," added Willy.

"That's exactly right." Rosy nodded. "Only by the grace of God can you beat something like this, Laura. His strength is made perfect in weakness."

"Well, I've got plenty of weakness," confessed Laura.

"Between you, Allie, and me, I always thought you were the strongest one," I told her.

"Yeah, I suppose there was a time when I thought that too." She smiled a sheepish little smile. "Guess I proved myself wrong about that."

"So, what do you think, Willy?" I asked. "Is it worth the risk to go on tomorrow night?"

He rubbed his chin. "Good question. Is it?"

"What have we got to lose?" asked Allie.

"Just our pride," I answered. "And that's not such a great thing anyway."

"That's right, baby. Pride comes before the fall, you know."

"I've certainly proved that, Rosy," said Laura.

"How about if we see how practice goes tomorrow," suggested Willy. "If Laura can hang in there and keep up, then I'll be convinced that it's worth a try."

"What about Iron Cross?" I asked. "Should we let them know what's up?"

"I think it's only fair. But first I'd like to call Eric Green and let him know what's going on.

Are you okay with that, Laura?"

She stiffened slightly, and I could tell she was still beating herself up about everything. "Yeah, it seems only fair. But I hate to think that I'm going to be the cause of a canceled contract." She choked up again. "I'm just so sorry about everything, you guys. Really, I am."

"We know, Laura," Willy said in an even voice. "And you've got to believe that we all forgive you. Now as your manager, I want you to take it easy today. Just rest up and eat right and take those vitamins that Elise got for you girls. We'll just have to cross that next bridge when we get there."

So that's what Laura did on the road today. She took a couple of naps, and I noticed she was reading her Bible a lot. Then she sat up with Rosy for a while, and the two of them appeared to have a good chat. Already, she seems a little more like the old Laura—in a very fragile sort of way. Will she ever be that strong, resilient Laura that I used to know? I sure hope so. And that's what I'm praying for.

RESTORATION

You made us and shaped us
we're formed by Your hand
You breathed Your life in us
a life that You've planned
You knew that we'd blow it

and fall on our face
and that we'd need Jesus
and Your loving grace
You remake, reshape us
with care You restore
our hearts and our spirits
till we're something more
till we're something bigger
and better—like new
till we reflect Your love
and look just like You

cm

Nineteen

Sunday, December 19

Somehow, by the grace of God, Redemption managed to pull it off in Hartford last night. Laura, although not in perfect form, handled herself in a professional and dignified manner. As a result, Michael White was not forced to jump in and rescue us.

Our practice yesterday morning had gone smoothly, and we'd met with Iron Cross in the afternoon to come clean on our "little problem," which really isn't little. Amazingly, a cool and composed Laura did most of the speaking.

"I'm sure you guys suspected that all was not well with Redemption," she said after she'd finished explaining everything to them. "And believe me, I take 100 percent of the blame for that. I've already told my band how sorry I am, and now I'm telling you guys. I am really, really sorry. I doubt if I'll ever be able to express how much regret I feel. And I hope and pray that you guys can forgive me. But I wouldn't blame you if you don't want us to open for you anymore."

Laura glanced over to where Allie and I were

sitting and sighed sadly. "Anyway, Willy has already told Eric Green about the whole thing, and he's supposed to get back to us later today. Right, Willy?"

"That's right. Eric's been calling the bigwigs to find out what they want us to do. Naturally, it's difficult reaching everyone on a Sunday. The girls are more than willing to open for you tonight, but they'll understand if you're concerned."

Allie grabbed my hand and squeezed it hard. I could tell she was as nervous as I was as we waited for Iron Cross to respond to Laura's confession. Laura went over and sat by herself in a corner. She sat up straight and watched the rest of the group, but the expression on her face was truly tragic. Right then and there I wanted to tell her how much I admired how brave she'd been in admitting her problem to these guys, and I could tell she felt absolutely rotten, but I also knew it wasn't the right time and place yet. It was that moment when it occurred to me that no matter how badly she had hurt our band—maybe to the point of dissolution—she had hurt herself far more. My heart really went out to her.

Willy continued in a solemn voice. "But I have to reassure you guys that the girls' practice sounded just fine this morning, and I don't believe they'll have any problems tonight. Still, you guys have a definite say in all this."

Now the room got so quiet that I could hear myself breathing. I closed my eyes and silently prayed for God to have mercy on Laura...and our band.

Then Jeremy cleared his throat. "Well, this is interesting. We didn't want to say anything, but we did have our suspicions about Laura." He glanced over to his brother before he continued. "Actually, it was Isaiah who felt something was wrong. The rest of us weren't too sure, well, until that last performance. Then we figured Isaiah was probably right." Jeremy put his hand on his brother's shoulder. "Okay, bro, why don't you say a few words. I'm sure you can speak for Iron Cross." The other guys nodded, so it seemed unanimous that Isaiah was the spokesman. This struck me as slightly odd since Jeremy is really the leader of the band, but I leaned forward in my chair to listen.

Isaiah stood up now and looked around the room, then finally stopped his gaze where Laura was still sitting by herself in the corner. Poor Laura. I could almost feel her cringing in her skin, and I'm sure she wished that she could just vanish about then. But I must respect the way she returned his gaze. Not in a cocky way, but just openly—as if she was waiting for him to really lay into her. As if she thought she deserved it. And maybe she did.

"Laura," Isaiah said in a gentle voice. "I suspected you were using at least a month ago. But at the same time, I wasn't absolutely certain. I guess I couldn't quite believe a level-headed person like yourself could fall into that pit of deception. I should've known better."

Laura nodded, and I could tell she was holding back tears. "Hang in there," I wanted to tell her.

Isaiah continued. "But the reason I could tell you were using is because I've been in the very same boat myself."

Laura's big brown eyes got even bigger, and I'm sure I saw her jaw drop just slightly, but she remained silent.

"But you're lucky, Laura—I should probably say blessed—that you realized what a trap you'd fallen into after only three months. It took me nearly a year. These guys can attest to that." Isaiah sighed as if even the memory was painful. "I really messed up big-time. Man, I thought I was such a pro at covering it up, and maybe I was at first, but it started to show up in my performance, not to mention my attitude. The worst was how it totally devoured my spiritual life. I felt dead for most of that year." He shook his head. "It was a cruddy way to live. But finally these guys figured out what was going on and confronted me. At first I denied everything, but it didn't take long for God to get hold of my heart again. And then I confessed, and these guys stood by me and helped me to get and stay clean. In a way I owe my life to them almost as much as I owe it to God."

Laura still looked stunned. "Really, Isaiah? That's really true?"

He smiled as he walked over to her. "That's right. So, if you're expecting us to judge or condemn you, well, you can just forget about it. Believe me, I would be the last one to cast a stone at anyone messed up by drugs." He took her hand now and made her stand up. "It took a lot of guts for you to come clean like this, Laura. And believe me, we respect you for it." He glanced back at his band. "Right, guys?"

Naturally, they all agreed. Then Isaiah gave Laura a big hug that was followed up by the rest of the guys in the band.

"Okay," said Jeremy. "Let's do a quick vote. Everyone in favor of having Redemption open for us tonight say 'amen.'" A resounding "amen" reverberated through the room, and then they launched into the old "Lilies of the Valley" amen song. Happy and relieved and tearful, we all joined in.

It wasn't until it was almost time to go onstage that Eric finally called Willy on his cell phone. Apparently he'd been unable to get a complete consensus from the bigwigs, but he told

Willy that we'd better go ahead and perform as
planned and that we'd sort it all out on Monday.

So, while our performance probably wouldn't
get the most stunning review in the music critics'
columns, it was solid and professional. Jeremy
said that we sounded better than ever, but that
was probably a kind exaggeration on his part.
Still, it's a relief to have this night behind us.
Now we need to hear Omega's opinion on this whole
thing. Needless to say, we are all praying.
Including Iron Cross. After the concert they
made a special point to tell us that they hoped
we'd get to continue opening for them.

"You girls are the most talented band we've
ever toured with," said Jeremy.

"Besides that, you're cute," Brett added with a
wink.

"Yeah, and I think we really get each other."
Isaiah gave Laura a sideways, brotherly hug. "We
understand that we're not perfect but are being
perfected by God."

"Yeah," said Michael. "And thanks to you, I can
say that I actually played in a chick band once."

We all laughed at that.

"Well, it's in God's hands," I told them.

"We'll be praying that Omega sees it that way,"
said Jeremy.

So now it's the waiting game again. But I'm
starting to think that this is just the way life

is—always something to wait for. I guess mostly I
need to be waiting on God.

WAITING GAME
flying along at a breakneck pace
running like crazy in this rat race
thinking you're early and finding you're late
before you know it, it's time to wait...
the waiting game
always the same
rules don't bend
will it ever end?
sitting for days with heads hung low
time stands still and clocks are slow
answerless questions hang in the air
don't you move, don't you dare
the waiting game
always the same
rules don't bend
will it ever end?
come to God, just fall on your face
beg for mercy and plead for grace
wait on Him with an honest heart
and soon He'll give a fresh start
the waiting game
God's always the same
don't curse the wait
the end is great
cm

Twenty

Tuesday, December 21

(CONFESSIONS IN PHILADELPHIA)

As it turned out, Omega was willing to give Redemption a second chance. I'm sure this had a lot to do with Iron Cross pleading on our behalf. And of course, God's great mercy.

But they had two conditions: 1) that Laura goes into some sort of drug rehab therapy after we go back home for our much needed break, and 2) that Allie and I also attend some support group meetings for friends and family members of addicts, like Al-Anon.

Since Willy is already involved in NA (Narcotics Anonymous), he'll help to get us all set up and make sure we faithfully attend our meetings. Not that we'd try to bail on him. We all agree that this is important. Not only for the sake of the band, but also for our own personal health and welfare.

But I guess the real surprise in all this—okay, the most recent surprise—is what Laura did at tonight's concert. It was a special Christmas concert that was actually being televised live on a Christian broadcasting network. Naturally, we'd already told our family and friends (when we were home for Thanksgiving) and, of course, encouraged everyone to tune in.

So just before the concert, right after we'd finished our regular PPP (preperformance prayer), it was time for the old rock-paper-scissors routine. But Laura asked if we'd mind if she gave her testimony tonight. Allie and I were both a little surprised, maybe even a little relieved since we knew we'd be on national TV, but we readily agreed. I didn't think much more about it since my focus was on delivering the best warm-up concert we've ever done. I really wanted to show Iron Cross as well as Omega that we could still do this. And so we did! Once again, Redemption rocked, and I think everyone was feeling pretty stoked.

It wasn't until the time came at the end of our performance that I realized how dicey this might get. I mean, it'd only been a week since Laura totally broke down onstage and had to be replaced by Michael. And despite her fantastic progress during the past few days, it occurred to me that this could happen again. In fact, when it was time to hand it over to Laura, I actually started to balk. But suddenly I got the strongest impression that God was behind this, so I introduced her.

"Now our bass player has something she'd like to say to everyone. Let's hear it for Laura Mitchell!" The crowd clapped, and I prayed as Laura stepped forward.

"Hey, everyone! Thanks for coming to hear us tonight." Laura smiled a nervous smile. "I'm really thankful to be here with you all. To be perfectly honest, I wasn't even sure if I would be allowed onto the stage tonight." She paused and the crowd got extra quiet. Clearly she'd gotten their attention. I glanced over to Allie, and I could tell by the look on her face that she was praying too. I prayed even harder now.

"I know you guys probably think that we've got it all together up here. I mean, here we are just singing about God and how He's touched our lives and everything. And believe me, that's all true. But we still have our problems." She took a deep breath. "And tonight I want to tell you about a pretty big problem that I recently allowed into my life—a problem that got bigger and bigger. And all because I quit trusting God."

She went on to dramatically explain how and why she first took the pills and how they slowly got a choke hold on her life until she couldn't even function without them. The crowd listened, spellbound. It was obvious they were shocked by her confession.

"The truth is, I had more faith in drugs than

I did in God. And it was killing me. Slowly but surely it sucked the life right out of me. And I have no doubt that if I'd continued along that path, I would soon be dead. Mostly because I just couldn't live with myself." She looked out over the crowd. "But here's the weirdest part about this whole thing. You see, I used to always be the one who sat in judgment against kids who messed with drugs. I mean, I had absolutely no tolerance, no grace, no mercy for anyone who was stupid enough to get involved with drugs. Can you believe that? And then it happened to me, and I came to realize that it could happen to anyone. And God showed me up close and personal that I had absolutely no right to judge anyone who gets caught in this kind of mess. My only responsibility is to love them and show them that God loves them even more. And so God, being kind and gracious, has really used a horrible part of my life to change me in an incredible way. I know I will never judge anyone for using again."

And then Laura stunned us all by giving a special invitation to any kids who were struggling with any form of addiction or drug abuse to raise their hands and to pray with her. I just totally lost it as Laura led them in the most beautiful prayer.

"Dear heavenly Father, we come to You now

knowing that You love us completely and unconditionally. And we confess to You that we are
blowing it." She paused, then directly addressed
the crowd. "Whatever your particular problem is
right now—whether it's drugs or alcohol or sex or
even cigarettes or food—place that burden in
your hands and lift it up to God." Then she continued with her hands lifted high. "We lift our
burdens to You now, Father God. We ask that You
take them from us, that You heal and forgive us.
We fall before You in humility and plead for Your
gentle mercy."

Then she paused for a couple of intense minutes before she finished. "We know that You're
here, Father. We know that You're listening to our
silent but heartfelt cries for help. We gratefully
accept Your forgiveness and ask that You'll help
us to forgive ourselves. And help us to follow You
with all our hearts from this day forward. Thank
You! Amen!"

The entire audience echoed her "amen," and it
felt as if God was right there in our midst. Not
that He isn't always here, but last night was an
intensity that I've never experienced before. The
crowd was hushed and obviously moved, and we
were all in tears as we exited the stage.

"That was totally amazing," Jeremy said as he
led his band out onto the stage. And instead of
hyping the crowd up like they would usually do,

Jeremy invited Isaiah to take a moment to speak as well. Isaiah backed up what Laura had said with his own brief testimony. And then they began their music with a moving worship song. They slowly built up into their regular rock-out style of concert in a crescendo that glorified God with every note.

I must say tonight was the most powerful thing I've ever participated in. And it seemed as if everyone felt the same way.

We were in the lobby until after midnight, signing CDs and posters as we encouraged and prayed with kids who had made a new commitment to God. And for the first time since our tour began, I don't recall being a bit uncomfortable or self-conscious with all of that intense one-on-one interaction. It felt perfectly normal. All in all, it was a truly awesome evening!

ALMIGHTY GOD
You've done it again
just blown us away
You've taken our darkness
and turned it to day
You transformed to good
what could've been bad
taken our misery
and made our hearts glad
You always amaze me

although You're the same
You redeemed us again, Lord
You remembered our names
Almighty God
we give You all praise
we give You our lives
for all of our days
amen!

Wednesday, December 22

(SHOPPING SPREE IN THE BIG APPLE!)

Mr. Sallinger's secretary from Omega surprised me with an early morning phone call today. Well, eight o'clock seemed pretty early because we'd been up so late the night before.

"Hello, Chloe," she said in a crisp business voice. "Mr. Sallinger would like to talk to you girls this morning. Can you get Allie and Laura to join you in your room?"

"Sure," I answered her in my froggy morning voice. "Give me a minute."

I gave Laura a shove, and she sat up in bed with wide eyes. It's amazing how much more alert she is now that she's not taking those stupid sleeping pills. "What's up?"

"The president of Omega Records wants to talk to us." I was already halfway through the door that adjoined Allie's family's room to ours.

"Hey, Al. Get in here. Mr. Sallinger is on the phone." I must admit to feeling nervous, worried that Omega could be upset by Laura's public confession to drug use last night. We hadn't warned anyone that she was going to do that. Who knew?

Soon we were all huddled around the phone receiver. "We're here," I told his secretary.

After a brief pause, Mr. Sallinger came on the phone. "Good morning, girls. Sorry to get you up so early. Did you have a pretty late night last night?"

"We got back to the hotel around one-thirty," I told him.

"Well, that was one great concert you girls participated in last night."

I could see the relief washing over Laura's face. "Thanks, Mr. Sallinger," I said. "Believe me, we were as touched as anyone."

"You and everyone else who tuned in to watch the show." He paused. "Laura, are you there?"

"Yes, sir."

"Well, little lady, you had most of my family in tears last night. And I promise you that's not something that happens every day."

"Thank you, sir, but that was God's doing," said Laura in a husky voice.

"Yes, you've got that right. But I just wanted to take a minute to tell you how proud you made us all, Laura. All you girls have been absolutely terrific on this tour. And to thank you, Omega has decided to send you to New York City for a little shopping spree and sight-seeing. Does that sound good to you girls?"

Naturally we all squealed with delight.

"And since we know you're all eager to get home," he continued. "We'll fly you back to save time. How does that sound?"

"It sounds great, Mr. Sallinger," I said.

"Good. Now Eric will be in touch with your manager to go over all the details. You girls have a Merry Christmas! And rest up during your break because, believe me, Omega's got some big plans for Redemption."

We thanked him and hung up then jumped around hugging and screaming. Davie joined in with us, although I'm sure he had no idea why we were so happy and relieved.

"I'm assuming you'll be needing your chaperone," said Elise with a grin.

Allie went over and hugged her. "Of course, Mom."

"Great, because I've always dreamed of shopping in New York City!"

We were checked out of that hotel and loaded onto the bus in a matter of minutes. Elise actually fixed us breakfast on the road. It was shortly afterward that Laura phoned her parents.

Naturally, she was pretty worried about their reactions to last night's public confession. We tried not to eavesdrop as she talked to her mom in the privacy of the bedroom. But it was easy to tell that it wasn't going too well.

"My mom's pretty upset," Laura told us when she finally emerged from the bedroom. "I guess she'd wanted me to keep quiet about the whole thing. But I told her that I've got to speak the truth the way I believe God is telling me."

"That's right and true," said Elise. "And as parents we should want that for our kids. Unfortunately, it's not always easy."

"Yeah." Laura slumped onto the couch.

"Don't worry," I said as I sat beside her. "I've seen your mom get over stuff before. She's really good at springing back."

Laura nodded. "I guess you're right."

"Besides," added Allie. "There's nothing you can do about that now. You'll have plenty of time to sort it all out when we get home."

By noon, Rosy dropped us off at our ritzy hotel smack in the middle of the city. We were sad to tell her good-bye, but we knew she was eager to get home for Christmas since she'd promised to join her brother's family in Virginia. We threw our bags in our rooms, ate a quick lunch, and were soon parading our stuff through one of the best shopping districts in the world!

Mr. Sallinger wired each of us a special bonus to be used for Christmas shopping. Willy offered to take Davie so Elise could "be just one of the girls," and the four of us set out to conquer New York. For what seemed like a whole a lot of money, we somehow managed to spend most of it! All in all, it was a whirlwind sort of day. But man, was it fun.

However, we didn't use all the money for presents. In the midst of our wild and crazy shopping day, Allie noticed a Salvation Army bell ringer in front of a swanky shoe store. She reached into her wallet, pulled out a pretty huge chunk of change, and dropped it into the locking iron pot.

The white-haired woman stopped ringing the bell for a moment as her eyes popped open wide. She studied Allie as if she'd come down from another planet. Then Laura and I, challenged by Allie's sweet generosity, quickly followed suit and the poor bell-ringing woman nearly toppled over with shock.

"God bless you!" we all yelled.

The woman smiled big. "And God bless you too!"

"Oh, He has!" called out Laura.

Our arms filled with bags and boxes—I've never had such fabulous gifts for my family and friends—we finally hailed a taxi and returned to our hotel. Amid my purchases are some gold charm bracelets I found at Tiffany's of all places. Two are for Laura and Allie and one is for Caitlin. I got some music charms and a couple other things that I know Laura and Allie will love. But for Caitlin's I just got an angel. At first I wasn't even sure why I picked an angel. It's not that I think Caitlin's an angel exactly, and yet she was like God's messenger to me at a time when I really needed to know that He loved me. And I know that angels are messengers from God. So maybe she is sort of an angel. Anyway, it was cool getting gifts that feel really special.

We caught up with Willy by dinnertime. He'd spent most of the day getting our airline tickets and taking care of all the general managing details as well as hanging with Davie, who appeared to be happily exhausted since he literally fell asleep in his soup.

Then Willy announced that, compliments of Omega, we were being treated to a Broadway show. We couldn't believe it. Willy had already lined up a babysitter for Davie in case Elise wanted to go too, which she did, and we all dressed to the nines (whatever that is) and rode the hotel limo to the theater district.

Now talk about your dream day. It was spectacular! Tomorrow we fly out, first class, and should be home in time for dinner. Oh, what a life!

HEAVEN
God, You are so good
You fill life with such pleasures
it's hard to imagine heaven
much finer with its treasures
but then i pause to think
of exactly what i'll do
when i walk into heaven
all i'll want is You
i'll fall down at Your feet
and thank You for Your grace
i'll worship and adore You
and i'll gaze into Your face
i'll sing to You my praises
i'll give You all my love
and earth will be diminished
by Your glory that's above
cm

Twenty-One

Thursday, December 23

(HEADING HOME FOR THE HOLIDAYS)

We actually sang "I'll Be Home for Christmas" as we waited in the never-ending security line at JFK Airport. A cappella, of course. But the weary holiday travelers cheered and applauded and even begged for more. So we sang a couple more Christmas carols, and before we knew it we were at the gate.

But as we were waiting for our flight, my cell phone rang. When I answered it, I was surprised to hear Josh's voice. And he sounded excited.

"Hey, what's up big brother?"

"You're not going to believe this!"

"What?" I couldn't tell by the tone of his voice whether it was good or bad, and I immediately became worried about my parents. "Is everyone okay?"

"Yeah. It's just that this is so amazing I don't know where to begin."

"You're getting married!" I shouted.

"No, no." He laughed. "That's definitely not it."

"All right then, you better tell me."

"Well, you know we saw your concert the other

night, which was, by the way, absolutely fantastic. Tell Laura that I've never been more proud of
her. She's quite a girl."

"Yeah." I winked at Laura who was balancing
her carry-ons and holding on to Davie's hand
while Allie and Elise searched the gift shop for
the latest fashion magazines and goodies. "We
think Laura's pretty special too. But is that why
you're so excited?"

"Nooo. The thing is, Caleb called yesterday. I'd
barely gotten home from school when I heard the
phone ringing. I was totally shocked to hear his
voice on the other end. Now, get this: Somehow our
brother managed to tune in to a certain concert
that was on TV on a certain night. Do you get what
I'm saying, Chloe?"

"No way!" My heart started to pound with
excitement. "He didn't!"

"Yes, he did! Get this, he and some friends were
just hanging, and apparently someone was channel surfing and had stopped to hear this
cool-looking chick band that was really rockin'
out. I think that's almost exactly how Caleb put
it."

"You are kidding!" My eyes were starting to
fill up now.

"I know; I know. It's incredible. And then Caleb
goes, 'Hey, I think that's my baby sister playing
lead guitar.' Well, naturally his friends don't

believe him. So he makes them leave it ON that gospel channel so he can prove to them—and himself—that it's really you. He admitted that he couldn't quite believe it either. He was amazed that you're all grown up."

"Josh, I think I need to sit down," I said, which was true. I was so dumbfounded that something this incredible could really happen. I collapsed onto a hard vinyl seat and just took in a deep breath. "Okay, continue."

"So anyway, he and his buddies watched the whole concert, Chloe. The WHOLE thing! Can you believe it?"

"No way!"

"Yeah. And the stuff that Laura and Isaiah shared actually touched Caleb. He said that he's known for some time that his life is a total mess, and he wants out but just isn't sure what to do next. Can you believe it? You girls actually managed to touch Caleb Miller's life."

"I am totally stunned, Josh. It sounds too good to be true. So what's going to happen now? And where is Caleb living anyway? Can he come home for Christmas?"

"Slow down, little sister. Okay, first of all, he's living in Mason—"

"Mason? That's only an hour from home. I thought for sure he was far away like LA or New York or something."

"I thought so too. And the parents said it's okay for Caleb to come home if he's serious about wanting to change."

"Well, that's pretty hard to judge, isn't it?" The last thing I wanted to see was another repeat of my father jumping all over Caleb on Christmas Eve. Ugh, I'd rather be stuck in an airport somewhere than live through that again.

"Yeah, but I think I convinced them that the only way we can know is to welcome him home and talk to him. I also reminded them of the prodigal son story. I think that got to them a little."

"So, he's really coming home then?"

"He'll be here tomorrow. He really wants to talk to you, Chloe."

I swallowed hard. "I want to talk to him too, Josh."

"I told him that. I told him that you'd been thinking about him a lot and praying for him. He thought that was pretty cool."

So, now I'm sitting on the plane counting the minutes until we land. Josh is picking me up at the airport, and for some reason, I feel more eager than ever to see my family again—all of them!

PRAISE GOD!
You are amazing, God!
way cool, amazing!

sometimes it feels so
dark and hopeless...
i feel like giving up
and then You burst forth
with a real live miracle
thank You! thank You! thank You!
praise You! praise You! praise You!
for what You're doing with Caleb
and for all Your grace and mercy
i place him in Your hands
Your amazing, loving hands
and i praise You! praise You! praise You!
amen!

Twenty-Two

Friday, December 24

(FAMILY REUNION)

When I got home last night, I could tell my parents were on edge about Caleb's out-of-the-blue visit. But at the same time, I sensed an unexpected hopefulness in both of them. And I guess I began to realize that they're not really the enemies here. They've been hurting as much, maybe even more, than I. Now I don't know why that never occurred to me before. Maybe I'm actually growing up.

Anyway, Caleb had told Josh that he'd be here in time for dinner tonight. And my parents decided that it might be best just to have a quiet evening with the five of us. So they've put off the larger gathering of family and friends until tomorrow. I think that was wise.

So Caleb finally shows up around five. It's already fairly dark outside, and I'm steadily checking out the kitchen window until I finally see what looks like an old beater car pulling up in front of the house. Then a scrawny-looking character, who I'm sure must be my older brother, reaches into the backseat and emerges with a cardboard box. Is that his laundry? I can tell by the way he walks that he's nervous, so I decide not to announce to everyone that he's here. Instead, I slip out the door and go to meet him, waving from the sidewalk.

"Hey, Chloe," he says with the same sweet smile that I would recognize anywhere. Never mind that his cheeks look slightly hollow and his skin is pale, although it could be the streetlight.

"Hey, Caleb." I run forward now and grab him into a hug, slightly crunching his cardboard box. Then I step back, suddenly self-conscious. "Sorry. Did I mess up your box?"

He laughs. "Nah, it's okay." Then he reaches out and roughs up my hair. "Cool hair."

I smile. "Thanks." I notice that his dark brown hair is long and matted and looks like it hasn't been washed in a while. "Going for dreadlocks?"

He laughs and pats his head. "Yeah, something low maintenance."

"I hear ya."

"Man, you've really grown up, Chloe girl." He nods with approval. "You're a good-looking young woman."

I laugh. "Not everyone would agree with you."

"I'll bet Mom had a cow when you got those piercings."

I take him by the arm and lead him toward the

house. "I think I've probably contributed a lot of gray hairs to both our poor parents." Then in a lowered voice I say, "Although Mom gets hers colored now."

"Nah. I'm sure I can take credit for any gray hair in this family. I've really been a mess."

"Hey, we've all messed up, Caleb. You heard my friends on TV the other night. Even when you mess up, there's still hope."

We're on the porch now, and he looks down at me with those puppy dog brown eyes. "You really think so?"

"I know so."

He shakes his head. "Man, you're quite a girl, Chloe."

Now I can't say it was all smooth sailing last night, but I could tell my parents were doing their best to be civilized. And I know that some of Caleb's answers were disturbing to them. His choice of lifestyle is, shall I say, slightly unconventional compared to theirs.

Basically, he lives with a group of people who work when they feel like it. Some are creative sorts, like Caleb, who enjoys creating things out of wood, and others I assume are just slackers who pass their time trying to figure out ways to get high. Now, these are just the deductions I made based on Caleb's comments, and I could be completely wrong. It seems Caleb has had a variety of jobs over the years, from washing dishes to pumping gas to things he said he'd rather not talk about. I can only imagine. But my take on him is that he's burnt-out and tired and very, very sad. I think he's ready for help.

"So, where do you go from here, Caleb?" Dad asks as we're finishing up dinner. "Any plans?"

Caleb just shrugs. "Good meal, Mom."

My mom smiles. "Thanks."

"I'm not trying to pressure you," my dad continues. "I'm just curious."

"You know, Dad," begins Josh, "It might be premature to ask Caleb about his future right now. Sometimes you just have to figure out the day in front of you."

Caleb nods. "Yeah, that's kinda how I feel."

"So, Caleb," continues Josh. "Do you feel as though you'd like to be clean today?"

Caleb seems to seriously consider this. "You know, that's not a question I want to answer lightly. And I don't want to give an answer just because I know that's what you're hoping to hear. But the truth is, I'm sick of my life. And even though it seems impossible—since I've tried before—I'd still like to change."

My dad brightens. "So, do you want to go back to school?"

Caleb holds up his hands. "I don't know about that."

"See," said Josh. "I think that's moving too far ahead again, Dad."

My dad frowns now. "But if you want to change your life, shouldn't you plan for your future? What better way to change than to go back to school?"

"I think there's a better way," I say quietly. "I think Caleb needs to surrender his life to God first."

"I agree," says Josh in a firm but gentle voice.

"Man, this is really something," Caleb says with a funny grin. "When did this family get so doggoned religious?"

"We used to take you kids to church." Mom's voice is slightly defensive.

"That's right," says Dad. "In fact, your mother and I met in a church youth group back in high school."

"No way," I say. My parents have never exactly struck me as the church youth group types.

"It's the truth," continues my mom with a slightly guilty expression. "I used to consider myself a strong Christian. Sort of like you, Chloe."

"Seriously?" This comes from Josh, and I can tell he's as confused as I am.

"We used to go to church three times a week," adds Dad as if his memory is suddenly kicking in. "Unfortunately, it wasn't the best church."

Mom nods. "It was a little, well, I guess you'd say overly fundamental. They were good people, but the rules could be almost overwhelming."

My dad holds up his finger to make a point. "In fact, one of their rules was that all children must be named from the Bible."

"Caleb and Josh," I say since I'm familiar with that part of the Old Testament.

"But we left the church before having Chloe," says Mom proudly. "Her name was part of our rebellion."

Josh laughs now. "Sorry, Mom, but there's a Chloe in the Bible too."

"Really?" She looks disappointed. But I feel pleased and decide I'll have to look it up later.

So on we go for more than an hour, just talking around the table like an almost normal family (although I'm not sure that such a thing really exists). Still, it was kind of fun. Not to mention eye-opening.

Finally, Mom begs us to lighten up on the "religious conversation" as she calls it. "Remember, it's Christmas Eve," she says in a cheerful voice. "And the Millers usually open presents on Christmas Eve. Josh, why don't you put on some Christmas music? I've even made some treats and things."

"Want some help in the kitchen?" I manage to offer as I control myself from saying what's really on my mind. Like, "Yeah, it IS Christmas Eve and when's a better time to talk about 'religious things'?" But, somehow, I keep this to myself. Maybe it's a God-thing.

Mom grins. "If the successful rock star isn't afraid to get her hands dirty."

I force a smile and bite my tongue, amazing myself once again at my restraint and self-control. However, to say I'm getting a little tired of her "rock star" routine would be a huge understatement. But this is Christmas, and I think I can handle it for another day or two.

Then we gather around the tree and prepare to exchange presents. Fortunately, I had time to pick something up for Caleb today—a dark blue North Face parka, which I have a feeling he could use after seeing his thin denim jacket. But suddenly I feel a little concerned over my somewhat over-the-top gifts. I don't want anyone to feel bad.

"If my gifts seem more extravagant than usual," I carefully explain, "It's only because the head of Omega was so pleased with our Christmas concert that he gave us bonuses and sent us off to New York City for a shopping spree."

"Cool," says Caleb. "I still can't believe how my baby sister has already hit the big time."

"Yeah," says Josh. "It kind of makes you feel like a loser."

"You're NOT a loser," I say indignantly. "See, this is just the reason I felt like I had to make a disclaimer about my gifts in the first place."

"Hey, don't apologize, baby sister," Josh says with a teasing grin. "I'm way open to getting a cool present from you. Bring it on!"

And so we begin exchanging gifts. My dad loves his cashmere sweater and pen set, and Mom surprises me by going on and on about her designer bag and scarf. I'm sure she can't believe her "unfashionable" daughter actually picked them out, but I knew it was her favorite designer. Josh loves his PalmPilot, and even Caleb seems pleased as he immediately tries on his new parka.

And I got some cool gifts too, but the one that means the most to me, the one I will treasure forever, is from Caleb. It's simply a wooden cross, carved out of a single piece of wood, with a leather string that makes it into a necklace. But it is more precious to me that gold and diamonds, and I plan to wear it during concerts.

"Thanks, Caleb," I tell him as I slip it over my head. "I really, really love it."

He smiles. "Cool. For some reason I'd started making it a long time ago, then sort of set it aside. But after I saw your concert, I decided to finish it up. I thought you might like it."

He was right. I do like it. I only hope and pray that the cross will one day mean as much to Caleb as it does to me. I know that he and Josh stayed up late tonight talking, I'm sure, about God's plan for salvation. And knowing Josh, Caleb will have heard the entire gospel before he goes to bed tonight. But that's great by me. I may have the gift of songwriting and singing, but Josh is definitely the preacher. Thank God!

THE MANGER AND THE CROSS
heaven's child
laid to rest
in a trough
God has blessed
a manger rough,
splintered, worn
God made flesh
when Christ is born
the child grows up
becomes a man
teaches, heals
fulfills God's plan
He shows pure love
forgives sin
shows us how
to enter in
but there are those
who doubt His fame
they question Him
they curse His name

on the cross
that God has blessed
He is killed
laid to rest
three days pass
and Jesus lives
love triumphs
He forgives!
cm

Twenty-Three

Saturday, December 25

I got up early this morning, feeling glad to be home and excited about spending more time with Caleb. But my hopes were quickly dashed when I discovered Josh sitting in the kitchen looking glum.

"What's up, Josh?"

He sighed. "Dad and Caleb kind of got into it last night."

I frowned. "Are they okay now?"

He shrugged. "Caleb took off."

I slumped into a bar stool and leaned my elbow on the counter. "What happened?" I asked in a flat voice.

"Well, Caleb and I talked until after midnight, and it was going pretty good. I think God is really nailing him, Chloe. He seems as if he's truly considering making a commitment."

"Cool." I sat up straighter. "So what went wrong?"

"Apparently Caleb wanted to smoke a joint before bed. 'To help him relax,' he said. Naturally Dad caught him and they got into it."

I groaned and let my head fall onto the granite countertop with a slightly painful thud.

Josh patted me on the shoulder. "Hey, don't take it so hard. You know as well as anyone that stuff like this just happens. And God can use it to remind Caleb that he really needs to change."

"Yeah, from the inside out." I sat up and rubbed my forehead. "I wish Dad could just love Caleb unconditionally."

"I think he does," said Josh. "It's just that he feels responsible for his family, you know? And he doesn't want any of us doing anything stupid or illegal under his roof. It's pretty understandable."

"I guess. But I'm still bummed. I was looking forward to staying in contact with Caleb."

"That's no problem. I've got his address and phone number. I told him that you and I will both want to be in touch."

I brightened. "Really? Did that cheer him up at all?"

Josh nodded. "Yeah, I think it meant a lot to him. I also gave him my old Bible and told him that we'll be praying for him."

I reached over and hugged Josh. "I love you so much, bro!"

He grinned. "Cool. I want my rich rock star sister to think I'm the greatest."

I frowned and punched him in the arm. "You know, I'm getting a little sick of that 'rock star' stupidity. You know that I'm still just Chloe, your bratty little sister who used to drive you nuts not so many years ago."

"Oh, yeah, her."

Suddenly I noticed that Josh was fully dressed and actually looked pretty nice. "What are you all dressed up for? Is there a Christmas service today?"

He shook his head, then glanced at his watch. "No. I've just got a little errand to run this morning. I'll be back in time for Mom's famous brunch though."

I nodded. "I see. Does this little errand involve a certain pretty blond friend of mine?"

He grinned. "Maybe."

"Did you get Caitlin a Christmas present?"

"Maybe."

"Come on, Josh. Please tell me you didn't do anything like get her a ring. You know how badly that went last year."

He firmly shook his head. "I definitely didn't get her a ring. Believe me, I learned my lesson. I just got her a friendship gift. No big deal."

I laughed. "Yeah, no big deal."

Then he smiled sheepishly. "Hey, Chloe, I can't help how I feel about her. But I'm trusting you to keep your mouth shut, okay? No sense in rocking her boat."

"Well, tell her hi for me and that I'd like to

meet her for coffee and a catch-up chat."

He stood. "I'm sure she'll want to hear all about the little rock star's latest adventures." Then he laughed as he dashed out the door before I could properly punch him. Oh, brother!

TWO BROTHERS
one in darkness
one in light
one loves daytime
one craves night
two brothers...
one is weak
and one is strong
one is right
and one is wrong
two brothers...
hold them, Father,
in Your hand
help them both
to understand
two brothers...
that You forgive
both equally
and You love them
unconditionally
two brothers...
mine
cm

Monday, December 27

(HANGIN' AT THE PARADISO)

Caitlin and I planned to meet for coffee at the Paradiso this morning. But I want to get there before her so I can check out my old digs without any distraction. And I must admit it is cool being back in our friendly little town. I think I forgot how much I like it here as I ride my bike down Main Street.

So I walk into the coffee shop and just drink in that rich smell of coffee and pastry and sigh. I spy Mike and Jill Trapp behind the counter, but they don't see me until I'm halfway through the nearly empty room.

"Hey, there she is!" Mike springs out from behind the counter and grabs me into a big bear hug. "Our local celebrity!"

"How you doing, Chloe," calls Jill from her position on the big steamer.

"Okay," I say as I recover from Mike's exuberance. "At least I was before your husband accosted me."

"Sorry." Mike backs off with a big smile. "It's just so great to see you. How long are you gonna be sticking around this time?"

"Long enough for everyone to get totally sick of us. We're going back to school and are supposed to be here until spring break."

"Cool. Say, Chloe, I don't suppose you remember how I'm the one who first discovered you and all..."

I nod. "Of course I remember. But, man, that seems like such a long time ago now."

"And sooo..." He adjusts his dark green apron, then gets this funny little grin.

I lift my brows. "And so?" Suddenly I'm thinking how it sometimes feels as if everyone wants a piece of me. But then I remind myself, this is just Mike. He's cool.

"Well, I was thinking, Chloe... Since I kinda helped discover you and all...maybe your band would consider doing a gig here."

I laugh. "Of course, we'd do a gig here."

He sighs in mock relief. "When?"

"When do you want?"

"Anytime between now and March. You name the date."

"How about New Year's Eve?" calls Jill from behind the counter.

"Sure. Well, I'll have to check with Allie and Laura."

"How's Laura doing anyway?" asks Mike in a quieter voice.

"You saw the Christmas special?"

He nods and I fill him in on the latest.

"Hey, Chloe," calls Caitlin as she comes in. We hug and get our coffees before we find a corner table.

"You look good," she says as she takes off her jacket.

"Thanks. So do you." I take a quick jewelry inventory and control myself from asking her what Josh gave her for Christmas. Then I hand her a small blue box.

"What's this?"

I grin. "Just something I picked up in New York." Then I tell her about Omega's shopping spree and how fun it was as she opens the box to discover the charm bracelet with a golden angel charm on it.

"Chloe, this is so sweet." She puts the bracelet right onto her wrist and holds it up.

"Sorry there's only one charm. But the angel reminded me of you. God kind of used you as my angel, you know."

She smiles. "And now He's using you for so many people."

"I figured you could add other charms too, you know, for whatever." Then I tell her how I got ones just like it for Laura and Allie.

"How are they doing," she asks with a concerned expression.

"I haven't talked to Allie since we got home. They went to visit her grandma for the holidays. But I spoke to Laura last night, and she's doing okay, all things considered. Her mom's having a hard time though."

"I've been praying for Laura. I know it can't be easy." Caitlin takes a sip of her coffee.

"Yeah, her mom's always been a little concerned about the whole rock band thing. Now she's saying that Laura may have to quit. But we're all praying that it works out."

"Does that scare you?" she asks. "I mean, to think the band could actually be hurt by this?"

"Yeah. It's been kind of hanging over our heads off and on during the whole tour."

"You mean Laura's been using—?"

"No, not so much the drug thing, but just one thing or another keeps hitting us. I think I've finally gotten to the place where I have to keep giving it all back to God. I have to trust Him with our future or else I'll just go crazy."

"That makes sense. Good for you, Chloe."

"Did you hear that Caleb came home for Christmas Eve?"

Caitlin nods. "Josh told me. That's so cool."

"Well, mostly cool. I was sad that he left so abruptly."

"Yeah, but God's going to use that whole thing, Chloe. And at least you guys can stay in touch now."

It takes us about an hour to really catch up, and by then the coffee shop is starting to get busy and we keep getting interrupted by friends. Mostly mine, which seems odd considering I had so few just a year ago. Ah, the price of fame.

"Well," says Caitlin as we stand up. "I promised Ben that I'd take him to the mall to return some clothes my grandma in California got him. They're about three sizes too small."

"He must really be growing."

"Yeah, like a bean stalk."

"How's he doing?"

She shrugs. "I'm not so sure. He seems different lately. You could be praying for him, Chloe."

"You bet."

And so as I pedal my bike home, I pray for Benjamin O'Conner. I pray that God will get ahold of him and never let him go.

HOLD ON
get him, God,
and hold on tight
hold him fast
if he should fight
show him, God,
that You're the One
who made the earth
the stars and sun
get him, God,
and let him know
the way Your love
never lets go
amen

Twenty-Four

Thursday, December 30

(HOMETOWN HAPPENING)

It's all set. Redemption will perform at the Paradiso Café on New Year's Eve. Mike had posters up by Tuesday, and he says the word is spreading fast.

"There's going to be standing room only," he told me on the phone yesterday.

"How about a cover charge?" I suggested. Actually it was something I'd been thinking about since he'd asked.

"What? You girls aren't getting rich enough on your own?"

I laughed. "That's not it. I just thought maybe we could donate any profit to the homeless shelter in town. Our pastor mentioned that they're having a hard time this year."

"That's a great idea," he said. "I might even kick in a little myself. Thanks, Chloe. We all need a moral compass sometimes."

I sort of cringed at that. I mean, Mike and Jill aren't Christians and I want to witness to them, but I don't like the idea of them thinking I'm

some kind of saint. "Well, Jesus is my moral compass," I told him. "Otherwise, I'm sure I'd be
totally lost."

He laughed, but not in a mean way. "Good
point."

Then I called Laura and told her about the
idea to donate the proceeds.

"Hey, maybe Mom will let me play," she said
hopefully.

"Is she still pretty down on you?"

Laura sighed. "You can't really blame her,
Chloe. I blew it pretty bad out there."

"I know. And I'm not blaming her. I just wish
she could see how much you've changed—I mean in
good ways. I think the whole experience has made
you a much bigger person. More like Jesus."

"Thanks. But I don't think my mom sees it quite
like that."

"Yeah, I'm sure she's pretty worried." Then I
told Laura about what happened with Caleb.

"That's too bad."

"Well, good and bad. We're trying to believe it
could be a turning point in his life."

"Yeah, well, don't hold your breath."

"Are you speaking as an addict now? Or as old
doubtful Laura?"

She laughed then got more serious. "Actually,
I'm speaking as a recovering addict with a sister..."

"Oh, yeah. How's Christine doing? Did she come home for Christmas?"

"She's doing about the same as usual. She wanted to come home for Christmas, but my parents wouldn't let her. As soon as I got home, they insisted I tell them the whole ugly story of where exactly I'd gotten the pills. And when they heard that Christine was involved, they got really furious. I didn't want to rat on her, but I wanted to be honest with them. I need to regain their trust, you know? Still, I feel pretty guilty about Christine. I mean, it's not really her fault."

"Not totally, but she should take a little of the blame."

"I guess. Then she called yesterday. And guess what?"

"She's given her heart to the Lord?"

"I wish. No, she wanted to sell me more pills. I told her I was done with that—forever. I even told her how messed up I got because of it. Then she told me she was broke and needed money."

"Oh, no..." I felt bad for Laura. "What'd you say?"

"I told her I had a bunch of Mickey D-bucks that I'd give her."

I had to laugh at that.

"I also told her that I'm in an outpatient rehab program now."

"What'd she say about that?"

"She didn't believe me. She just hung up."

"I'm sorry, Laura."

"Yeah, me too."

"So, how's the old rehab going?"

"It's kind of cool. I mean, in a weird way. It's like I was getting so down on myself about the whole thing, thinking that I must be such a lowlife to get hooked. But hearing others talk about their addictions makes me feel like less of a loser. I'm starting to see that we're all wired differently, and some of us need to be really careful. I've also been able to share with them about how God has been key in my recovery."

"That's cool. Allie and I are going to attend our first Al-Anon meeting next Tuesday."

"I don't see why you guys need to—"

"Because we love you, Laura. And because we promised Omega. Remember?"

"I still can't believe all the trouble I've caused."

"So, do you think your mom will cool off when it's time to go back on tour?"

"Thank goodness we have almost three months. My dad's been trying to convince her that it was just a onetime blunder. I'm sure glad someone in this family believes in me."

"Oh, Laura, I'm sure your mom believes in you too. She's just very protective of her baby."

Laura made a groaning sound. "Thanks, I

needed that little reminder."

Then we joked about how we've been taking so much abuse for being the "rock stars" back in our old stomping ground.

"You know Allie would be eating this up," I said.

"When's she getting home anyway?"

"In time for tomorrow's gig."

"I guess we don't really need to practice."

"Nah, I think we can pull it off for the hometown crowd. But I'm hoping we can get back to practicing after the New Year." Now this is an understatement, since I had the old nightmare about flopping big-time on the stage. Still, I think it's too soon to crack the whip.

Tuesday, January 4

(CRUISING 'ROUND TOWN)

Where to begin? First off, most importantly, I now have wheels! Well, other than my bike, that is. It all started when I wanted to borrow a car for New Year's Eve.

"Why don't you get your own car?" suggested my dad as he made coffee that morning.

I frowned at him and got ready to argue, but then it hit me—why don't I get my own car?

I knew he could see the light go on in my face about then. "You see, not such a bad idea from the geezer, eh? If you had your own car we wouldn't always be scrambling for rides around here."

"Yeah," I said slowly. "And I could actually afford it too. Do you really think it's a good idea?"

He grinned. "I can't believe you're asking me that. Since when have any of us been able to tell you what to do?"

"Hey, I'm trying to be an obedient and submissive daughter now."

He just laughed. "Well, as fate would have it, I don't have to work today. You want to go looking, pumpkin?"

"Looking for what?" asked Josh as he emerged looking half awake.

"Your sister's new car!"

"Hey, cool. Can I come?"

So the three of us went car shopping. My dad was certain that New Year's Eve—and it was just starting to snow—would be the perfect time to get a real deal. And as it turned out, he was right.

Naturally, Dad and Josh wanted to look at the hottest, fanciest wheels out there. It's like they think I'm made of money now. But I humored them. And we actually test drove a Mitsubishi Eclipse Spyder (Josh's suggestion). But the whole time I kept eyeing the back lots for what I really wanted. To say my brother and dad were a little let down when I finally saw the car of my dreams is a total understatement. But there it was—a completely refurbished 1972 Volkswagen bus. Now talk about a classic!

"You gotta be kidding," said Dad. "You want that old thing?"

I nodded with a big grin.

"I think I might've ridden in the back of that thing during my college days," Dad said with a frown. "I can't believe you could have the pick of the lot, and you want that."

Josh just laughed. "I think it suits you to a T, Chloe. Don't know why I didn't see it coming."

"Yeah. We can put all our band equipment in it and everything. Or even go camping. See, it's complete with a little fridge and everything."

My dad rolled his eyes. "A real deluxe edition."

"And the color is perfect," I said. "Green, like the earth."

Then my dad hugged me. "My little earth muffin. Well, I guess you better let me do the dickering—since I'm not the one who's in love with it."

And dicker he did. I got it for a real bargain. And it runs great too. Josh had to give me some lessons on how to handle a clutch. But by the time I needed to pick up Laura and Allie (I'd told them they were riding with me), I was driving like an old pro. Naturally, Laura thought I was nuts.

"Why did you want this old thing?" she asked as I helped her to load up her bass.

"I don't see why you're complaining," I said. "Look at all the gear we can get in here."

Fortunately, Allie saw it differently. "This is totally cool," she said as she checked out my fridge, already stocked with soda and snacks. "You want me to do some decorative painting on the outside? Like they did in the seventies?"

"That'd be cool," I said. "But I'll have to see sketches first."

Then we did our Paradiso gig, and it was a blast. It's amazing how easy it seemed after what we've been doing. It was more like jamming with friends than really performing. And we took lots of breaks and hung out. Mike told us that the evening managed to earn about five hundred dollars for the homeless shelter. Not bad.

Then tonight, Allie and I went to our first Al-Anon meeting. Okay, we felt a little weird at first because it was mostly older people and wives or parents of people with alcohol problems. But when the leader started explaining things like enabling and codependency, I started paying attention. Not so much for Laura, but I was thinking about Caleb. I know how much I'd like to help him change—and that's not bad—but until he wants to change for himself, my efforts would be useless. Perhaps even harmful.

"Addicts need to feel the pain of their own natural consequences," the leader said. "The more they are protected from the results of their bad decisions, the longer it will take them to realize they need help."

And so I'm praying that Caleb will feel the pain of his bad choices. I don't want God to kill him or anything. But a slap across the side of the head probably wouldn't hurt.

BRING HIM LOW
smack him down, God,
let him feel the pain
show him his loss
so he'll want the gain
knock him low, Lord,
flat in the dirt
till he begs 'mercy!'
let him feel the hurt
let him grovel
crawling in shame
let him feel like crud
till he cries Your name
then lift him up, God,
give him Your grace
bandage his wounds
let him see Your face
amen and amen

Twenty-Five

Friday, January 7

(FIRST WEEK IN SCHOOL)

It felt pretty weird to be back in school again. Kind of knocks you down a peg or two when your biology teacher throws a pop quiz that you're totally unprepared for. But such is life.

After the first few days, our friends started treating us like normal again. Well, other than Tiffany Knight who likes to glom on to me as if I were free ice cream. And maybe that's partly my fault because I was trying to be polite by answering her numerous e-mails while we were on the road. Actually, I tried to answer everyone's. But for some reason, Tiffany assumes that means we're best buds now. I'm sure she thinks it will help her popularity status, since she's been a lot more on the outside of things this year. Even Kerry treats her like she's got poison ivy.

Actually, I think Tiffany's meanness has finally caught up with her. Not that she's being so terribly mean these days, well, not so you'd notice. Although I did catch her making a fat comment about Marty Ruez today in the cafeteria. Naturally, I didn't let that comment fly. I think

Tiffany had almost forgotten what a tough chick I can still be sometimes.

"How would you feel if someone said something like that about you?" I asked Tiffany point-blank at the drink machine. I've decided that I'm not the least worried about offending her—as long as what I'm saying is honest and not mean-spirited. I actually thought I might be able to drive her away earlier this week by talking about God and preaching at her a lot more. But so far that hasn't worked.

"What do you mean?" She looked at me with what I'm sure she must think are innocent blue eyes.

"I mean, how would _you_ like someone to make a nasty comment about your appearance?" I said as Allie's elbow jabbed me in the ribs. She thinks I should try to ignore Tiffany.

"What's wrong with my appearance?" asked Tiffany.

"Well, you're not perfect, you know. We all have our flaws, but no one likes to hear them publicly announced in the cafeteria."

"I just said what everyone knows is true. Someone like Marty Ruez should avoid things like greasy pizza and fries."

"And who made you the diet police?" I jabbed a straw into my soda.

She just shrugged.

I picked up my tray. "All I'm saying, Tiffany, is

that Jesus wants us to love everyone as much as we love ourselves. And I have a feeling you love yourself pretty good." I glanced at her designer threads and perfectly styled hair and makeup. It probably takes this girl a good two hours to get ready for school every morning.

"Hey, Marty," I called, hurrying to catch her. "You want to sit with us today?"

Her face brightened with a smile. "Sure." Then she noticed Tiffany coming behind me. I've never actually invited Tiffany to sit with me, but so far it's made no difference. "Oh, maybe not..."

"Hey, don't worry about her," I whispered. "If she gets out of hand, we'll just preach at her."

Marty laughed then followed me over to a table where Allie was just joining Cesar, Jake, Spencer, and Marissa. We've been trying to sit with different kids every day. Part of our reach-out campaign at Harrison High. But today Laura said she wanted to sit with her old friends. And Allie and I decided to eat with Cesar and the rest. I wasn't quite sure how Tiffany would handle our little crowd of misfits, but it could prove interesting. And at least it might make her rethink this somewhat frustrating devotion she seems to have toward me.

"Mind if we join you?" I asked.

"Of course not," said Cesar. "Hey, Marty, how's it going?"

I glanced over my shoulder to see if Tiffany was intimidated by these guys, but she seemed undeterred. I sat next to Cesar and Marty sat next to me, forcing Tiffany to sit across the table beside Marissa who was eyeing our newcomer with open curiosity if not downright hostility.

"What's up with you?" Marissa asked Tiffany in a slightly challenging tone. "Don't you usually try to hang with the preppies? Or have you been completely kicked out of their snooty little club?"

"It's okay, Marissa," I said. "Tiffany's with me. And as far as I know this is a public place where people can sit where they like, right?"

Marissa scowled. "Oh, yeah, sure, Chloe. And I suppose I could march right over there and sit at the preppy table too. I'm sure they wouldn't say a thing about it either."

"Do you think the day will ever come when we can all get along?" Cesar asked with a longing tone.

"Yeah, in heaven," said Allie.

"Oh, great," said Marissa. "Here comes the sermon for the day."

Spencer rolled his eyes. "I think I'm gonna get me some fresh air."

"Haven't you given up that old line, Spence?" I asked. "Why not just call a spade a spade and say you're going out for a smoke?"

"Yeah, sure, I'm gonna announce that to God and everyone." He pushed back his chair.

"Why not?" said Allie. "And while you're at it, you could even admit that you're not smoking plain old tobacco either. Sheesh, it's not like everyone doesn't know it already."

I nodded. "And it's not like what we think matters to you anyway. In fact, the only way you'll ever quit will be when you finally realize it's just a great big stupid trap and get totally sick of it."

Allie's eyes lit up. "Hey, Spencer, did you know that Chloe and I are going to Al-Anon meetings now?"

"Al-Anon?" Spencer said with real interest. "You girls take up drinking on your big concert tour?" He laughed. "I heard that old Laura got herself hooked on drugs, but I know that can't be true."

I looked him in the eye now. "As a matter of fact, it is true. Laura did get hooked on amphetamines as well as sleeping pills. She even admitted it on national TV."

"You guys were really on national TV?" He looked slightly impressed now and had obviously missed my point.

"Where were you, Spencer?" injected Marissa. "I thought everyone in town watched that Jesus freak show."

"Yeah? Well, I was probably out partying." He grinned like he had some great secret to hide, like his drug life was something wonderful and exciting, even though we all knew otherwise.

"So what's up with Al-Anon?" asked Marissa. "Isn't that for alcoholics?"

"Actually, it's for friends and family of people with addiction problems. Allie and I agreed to go for Laura's sake, not that she'll ever fall into that crud again. But we promised our recording company that we'd attend those meetings while Laura's doing her drug rehab thing."

"You gotta be kidding," said Spencer. "You saying that Ms. Perfect Laura Mitchell is actually in an honest-to-goodness drug rehab program?"

I nodded.

He laughed even louder now, slapping his thigh for emphasis. "Now that's just way too funny."

"It's not that funny," I said in a flat voice. He was really starting to tick me off now.

"Hey, I'll bet Laura would give you a ride to one of her meetings, Spencer," said Allie. "Course, you'd probably be too chicken to go."

Spencer shook his head. "I don't need no stupid rehab program. If I wanna quit, I'll just quit. No big deal."

"It's not that easy," Jake said in a quiet voice.

"Oh, no." Spencer held his hands up like he

was scared. "I think I hear that sermon coming on now."

"Good for you, Jake." Allie slapped him on the back. "You go ahead and preach it, brother."

Jake grinned. "Yeah, well, I never would've gotten clean if it hadn't been for God in my life."

"Amen!" I said with a raised fist. I noticed how Tiffany looked fairly uncomfortable just then. I'm sure she probably wished she were sitting at some other table.

Spencer stood. "Oh, man, I'm like so outta here."

"And God can deliver you too, Spencer," continued Jake in an evangelistic sounding tone that almost made me laugh, although I knew Jake was perfectly serious.

Spencer backed away. "Thanks, but no thanks."

"We'll be praying for you, Spence," Allie said with a grin.

"Praying that you figure out how you're heading down a dead-end street," I added with a wink.

Spencer just frowned and shook his head. "Yeah, it's so nice having you Jesus freaks back at school," he said with dripping sarcasm.

Cesar laughed. "Hey, I'm happy to have some more backup."

"Me too," added Jake.

We joked and bantered some more with Marissa jumping in about where Spencer had left off. But

I don't think Tiffany said a single word during
the whole time. I halfway expected her to get up
and leave. And I'm sure she wondered what in the
world she was doing sitting there. But it was her
choice and her problem. At least she got to hear a
little wholesome preaching. And who knows where
that might lead.

Despite my mixed feelings for this girl, I
actually think that if she really invited Jesus
into her heart, she might start changing and
become a more tolerable person. Okay, I know I'm
supposed to love her in the same way that God
does—unconditionally. But the sad truth is, I
still need lots and lots of help with that chal-
lenge.

FOR NO REASON
in our despicable, hopeless, selfish existence
He loved us
for no reason
other than His nature
which is to love us
in our messed-up, loathsome,
clueless human condition
He loved us
for no reason
other than His nature
which is to love us
in our freaked-out, neurotic, desperate state

> He loved us
> for no reason
> other than His nature
> which is to love us
> can't we at least try to do the same?
>
> cm

Thursday, January 13

There's a winter dance tomorrow night, and Laura and Allie and I decided to go <u>without</u> dates! I remembered Caitlin telling me how she and Beanie and Jenny did the same thing once and had a really great time. (I think this was a piece of one of her nondating lectures.) Anyway, Laura and Allie both said they were game. Not all that surprising since Laura's still hoping that she and Ryan have a romantic future (he stopped by her house during Christmas break...), so she's not interested in any of the guys in high school.

And then, of course, Allie's still smitten with Brett, her beloved drummer boy from Iron Cross. They've been e-mailing each other pretty regularly. Actually, I'm thinking that's not such a bad thing since it keeps her from getting romantically involved with any guys at school. And believe me, she's had her chances. I remember how that proved such a disaster last summer, and I sure don't want to see that happen again. Not that

Allie would ever put herself in that kind of position again. And I'm sure that Brett wouldn't take
advantage of her the way that slimebucket Taylor
Russell did at the lake. But I suppose I still feel
kind of protective of her in that regard.

And then there's me. To be totally candid, in
the privacy of these pages, I'm still a little
dreamy over Jeremy (although I will admit this to
no one!), and I suppose I've gotten even worse
since being away from him. You know what they
say about absence and the heart... I suppose it's
true. And it's a bit ironic since I'd been feeling a
little like that about Cesar while we were on the
road. But now that I see him every day, my heart
has calmed down. A good thing too, as it turns
out, since he's still "kissing dating good-bye."

Actually, I admire how he's sticking to his
commitment. For him it seems to work. And I'm not
entirely sure that I shouldn't adopt the same
philosophy. Although I want my convictions to
come from God, not just my interest in some passing fad. For the moment, it's rather a nonissue for
me. Well, until I think about Jeremy, that is. Oh,
be still, my fickle heart!

But back to the dance thing. It was amazing
how quickly word got out about our joint stag
date, and now several others, including Cesar,
have asked if they can join in. So it looks as if
there's a whole bunch of us going stag, but

together. And I think it'll be fun. We just plan to hang out, eat junk food, and have a good time. Okay, I must admit to being a little disappointed when Tiffany announced that she wanted to join us too. How could I say no? I mean, what <u>would</u> Jesus do? Still, I feel like it'll take some of the fun out, and I know that's wrong. I know I need to love her, but the truth is: <u>I just wish she'd find another stinking friend!</u>

Sometimes I think that Tiffany Knight must be "my cross to bear." And I imagine myself dragging this opinionated, Tommy Hilfiger wearing, preppy girl throughout my life like a big old cross. Then I think that God must be sitting up there just laughing, thinking how much fun it is to mess with me like this. Naturally, He's only doing it for my own good—although it beats me how hanging with Tiffany can do me much good when it actually makes me want to cuss sometimes. (Something I thought I had conquered long ago.)

Still, I do think I've been doing a little better at loving her. Well, mostly. To be completely honest, I've found her to be especially aggravating lately since she keeps insisting that she's a Christian just because she's been going to her parents' church again. But when I asked her if she'd really given her heart to God, she got the blankest expression, like she didn't have a clue as to what I meant. Oh, well. Maybe in time.

On another note, we've been having lots of great band practices lately. Fortunately, Laura is still allowed to practice with us, although her mother has made it perfectly clear that she's having second and third and fourth thoughts about letting Laura go back on tour after our break. I try not to think about that too much. Instead, I just pray and pray and pray. Laura thinks it will all work out in the end. Her faith has really grown lately.

Still, I try to think positively, and I've been introducing some new songs these last couple of weeks. Some of them sound pretty cool. The encouraging thing is that all three of us are 100 percent committed to our music right now. And we all know that most of our spare time should go into some pretty serious practices, especially since we remain under contract.

Just the same, we try to carve out time for our "high school experience" too. Willy has really encouraged us in this area.

"You'll have more to sing about and minister from if you're living a life like the kids who listen to you perform," he told us just last week. "If you allow yourselves to become hermits and do nothing but music, you might lose your edge in really touching hearts."

I think that must be true. So we've made it a priority to go to ball games and dances and youth group and regular stuff. Just being your typical high school kids—whatever that is. And it's actually been pretty fun. It's surprising how much more you appreciate these everyday activities when you've been away for a while.

GOOD LIFE
life's about taking a chance
try to sing and learn to dance
laugh it up with happy friends
when you bicker make amends
thank the Lord for each new day
see what sparkles on the way
celebrate—it's great to live
feel the joy when you can give
help someone who's feeling down
don't be afraid to play the clown
find new ways to show real love
so your friends will look above
to the One who loves us so
live and laugh and love and grow
cm

Twenty-Six

Sunday, January 16

We had a blast at the dance. Even having Tiffany along wasn't so bad, although her dress was a little over the top. At least for our motley group. Allie and Laura and I wore retro outfits that we've used for concerts. No big deal. And Marissa sort of followed suit, although her look was more on the dark side with her black fishnets and thigh-high boots. But Tiffany wore a dress that looked like something from the red carpet at the Academy Awards. I was surprised she hadn't gotten herself a wrist corsage to complete the look. But just the same, we tried to be kind. Well, except for Marissa.

"What's with you, Tiff?" Marissa used her derogatory tone. "Looks like you wanna be prom queen or something."

"My mom picked it out," said Tiffany quickly.

"It's pretty," I tried, although I'm sure I sounded lame.

"Pretty weird," Marissa said with a quick roll of her eyes.

But it wasn't long before we forgot about clothes and just enjoyed laughing and talking and dancing with everyone in our group. We even had a group photo taken that I plan to hang in our tour bus when we hit the road again. That is, IF we hit the road. On our way home from the dance, Laura told me that her mom plans to call Omega next week and discuss "Laura's contractual obligations."

"I didn't want to tell you until after the dance," she said as I dropped her off at home.

"Thanks," I said halfheartedly.

"What does that mean?" asked Allie, the only other one left in the van by then. "Is your mom really pulling the plug?"

"I don't know. I've tried to talk to her about it, but she just closes up. Even my dad is frustrated."

"I don't see why parents should have such a big say in this," said Allie. "I mean, it's our lives and we're the ones doing the work."

"But we're not adults," I reminded her. "Besides, remember what Pastor Tony said about how God puts leaders in our lives so that He can guide us through them?"

"But it's confusing," said Laura. "Like who am I supposed to listen to when my parents don't agree on this? My dad's not totally okay with me going back on tour, but he's mostly supportive. Then at the same time, my mom's mostly opposed."

"That's tough," I told her. "My parents were

kind of divided last spring. My mom thought Omega would take unfair advantage of us, while my dad just thought it was a great opportunity. But she's pretty much come around."

"Guess I should be glad that my dad's so checked out," said Allie. "Sometimes it's easier having just one parent."

"Well, we'll just have to really pray for your mom," I told Laura.

"Would it help for Willy to be involved in that conversation?" asked Allie hopefully. "He's a good mediator."

"Yeah, maybe." Laura opened the door. "I'll give him a call and let him know what's up."

So we've all been praying for Laura's mom the last couple days. And we'll keep on praying throughout the week. I just wish there was something more we could do to convince her that Laura will be okay now. Of course, even as I write this, I realize that I might be praying selfishly. I mean, how can I guarantee that Laura won't have a problem as a result of our touring? Only God knows that for sure. So I must pray for His will—not mine. That's not going to be easy to do.

YOUR WILL
i admit i want things my way
and i think i know what's right

but my vision can get blurry
and my daytime could be night
i don't always know Your will, Lord,
or the way You'd have me go
i get tricked and i can stumble
many times i just don't know
so before i throw a tantrum
kick and scream, demand my way
i must come and bow before You
wait and listen as i pray
You alone know how to lead me
You alone know what is best
Your will alone is what i long for
it's in Your will that i can rest
amen

Tuesday, February 1

(WILD AND AMAZING TIMES)

It seems like Laura's mom has jerked us around,
back and forth, for nearly two weeks now. I feel
like a Ping-Pong ball or maybe it's a yo-yo with
all the ups and downs. Laura's mom did call
Omega, as threatened. But according to Laura,
the conversation seemed to go surprisingly well.
And Mrs. Mitchell seemed completely reassured
that everything was going to be okay and Laura
would be allowed to tour again. I'm sure we all
breathed a collective sigh of relief as we

thanked God for answering our prayers.

Then just a few days later, Laura's sister Christine was hospitalized for a methamphetamine overdose. Naturally, this sent Mrs. Mitchell into a complete tailspin. And who could really blame her? They thought Christine was going to die, and everyone was extremely upset. We had our whole church praying for her around the clock, and I barely slept the first couple of nights, I was praying so hard. But it was during this time that Laura's mom changed her mind. She decided that Laura would most definitely not be going back on the concert tour. She even called Omega and told them the sad news. It was a pretty dark hour for all of us. But at the time we were so focused on Christine and praying for her recovery that thoughts of Redemption and touring were pretty removed from our minds.

But finally after five long days, Christine miraculously pulled through and the doctors expect her to make it. Even more amazing was the change of her heart. Laura said that the whole thing was like a spiritual awakening for her sister. And Christine said she had seen heaven and come back for a second chance. Naturally, we're all crediting God and thanking Him for this incredible miracle. God is so amazing!

Of course, the Mitchells gladly welcomed their prodigal daughter back into their home to recuperate. Laura spent a lot of time sharing and praying with her older sister. She even invited Christine to a couple of our practices, and we all thought she was doing great. It was during this time that Mrs. Mitchell changed her mind again, saying that Laura could tour after all.

Then just a few days ago, Christine went missing, and the Mitchells totally freaked. Everyone looked all over town for her, but no one could find her. Naturally, Laura's mom had second thoughts about letting Laura go on tour again. But in defense of Mrs. Mitchell, she did apologize to all three of us yesterday when she invited us over to talk.

"I'm sure you girls must think I'm crazy," she said as she was literally wringing her hands. "But I feel it's a parent's responsibility to protect her children."

I nodded. "I can understand that."

"Thanks, Chloe. And your dad has told me a little about your situation with your older brother, so I'm sure you can understand how pdifficult this is."

"Yeah. Believe it or not, I really worry about Caleb too. But I'm trying to spend more of my energy praying for him now. Going to those Al-Anon classes has helped me to see there's nothing I can do to stop him from using. I can only pray for him and love him. But he's the one who has to want to change."

Mrs. Mitchell seemed to consider this. "Yes, I'm sure you're right. But it's so hard to just stand by and watch your own children throwing their lives away."

Laura sat up straighter. "Mom, I know I did something really, really stupid while we were touring last fall. But you know that I don't want to live like that. I hate the way I felt while I was taking those stupid pills, and I'll graduate from my rehab next week. I honestly don't think I'll ever make that mistake again."

"But how can you know?" said Mrs. Mitchell. "Look at your sister."

"I'm not my sister," Laura said with clenched fists. "I hate what Christine is doing to her life. Just watching her is enough to make me never want to mess with anything like that again. Can't you see that?"

"I can see that right now," said her mother. "But what about when you're on the road? Days and weeks go by and I don't see you. How am I supposed to—?" She started to cry now.

"But we see her, Mrs. Mitchell," I said. "And now that we know what happened and since Allie and I have been involved in Al-Anon, I think we know what to look for."

"That's true," agreed Allie. "And my mom and Willy and even Rosy know what's going on too.

They'll all be watching more carefully."

Laura nodded eagerly. "It's true, Mom. Even if I wanted to—and I don't—I couldn't get away with anything like that again."

Mrs. Mitchell wiped her eyes. "I'm sure what you're saying makes sense, baby. And maybe I'll see things differently once we find out what's going on with Christine. In the meantime, I guess you'll just have to be patient with me."

Now I stood up and walked over to where Mrs. Mitchell was sitting on the couch. And in a bold move that still surprises me, I asked if we could pray for her.

She blinked, then smiled. "Well, of course, if you really want to."

And all three of us stood up and put our hands on Mrs. Mitchell's shoulders, just the same as we've done when we've prayed for each other over a particularly challenging burden. Then we prayed that God would comfort her and give her peace and help her to trust Him with the outcome of not only Christine's, but also James's and Laura's lives.

"And please, God," continued Laura. "Help my mother to see that I am not like my sister, that my choices are based on my commitment to You, and that is a commitment I have vowed to keep."

We all said amen, and Laura's mother wiped her eyes again. She didn't make any promises. And

I suspect it's just as well since I don't think she knows exactly how she feels about all this yet. I do know that we're all praying for Christine.

And I must admit that all Christine has been through—and put us through—is a reminder that my own brother could be in just as much trouble too. I don't understand why people would willingly get themselves into something like this. Then I remember what happened with Laura, and I realize that drugs can be very sneaky. I suspect that Satan uses every trick in the book to get people hooked. And then I just feel mad!

KICK HIM, GOD
zap him, pound him, beat him down
nail the devil, make him drown
in his lies and in his hate
make him taste his fiery fate
kick him hard and grind him fast
give him pain and make it last
tie his hands and bind his feet
hold his behind to the heat
he's a thief and cheating liar
throw him in the pit of fire
that is what he has in store
silence him forevermore
cm

Sunday, February 6

(ENCOURAGING WORDS)

Christine finally returned home yesterday. "Totally burnt and wasted," according to Laura. She also said that her sister broke down and cried, confessing to her parents that she'd "fallen off the bandwagon" when she stopped by to "say hey" to a couple of her drug friends. Big surprise there. Of course, Laura also said that this wasn't terribly unusual with hard drug addicts.

"Still, it's sad," I said over the phone this afternoon.

"But without serious rehabilitation, she'll never be able to stay clean for long," said Laura. "At least that's what I've learned in my rehab class." She laughed, but there were tones of sadness in it. "It's so ironic that I'm the one in rehab."

"Did you tell Christine she needs rehab?"

"I've told both her and my parents. And I even offered to take her in and sign up. I'd even go to the classes with her if it would help."

"What'd she say?"

"At first she didn't think she needed it. But this time Christine said she thinks she might be ready for this."

"Really? Well, that's good."

"Yeah. But I tried to make it really clear to my

parents that it would be up to Christine to make her recovery work. I mean, I can take her to meetings and everything, and we can all encourage her, but she's got to want it for herself. I sure don't want my parents blaming me if it doesn't work out."

"Yeah, but they wouldn't do that."

"Probably not. But you know how my mom's been so wishy-washy about me going back on tour lately. I just wanted to lay all my cards on the table."

I thought for a moment. I wanted to say something encouraging, but I knew I needed to get it right. "You know, Laura," I began slowly. "You've been handling everything incredibly well. I'm proud of you."

"Huh?"

"I mean about the pills and everything. I just think you must be making God feel proud too."

There was a brief pause, then in a quiet voice she said, "You really think so?"

"Yeah! I do. I think you're pretty amazing."

She sighed. "Thanks, Chloe. You know sometimes, like in the middle of the night, I still beat myself up over that whole thing. I think how incredibly stupid I was, and like why did I do something so senseless, and if only I could do it all over again. You know, creepy stuff like that."

"You shouldn't be so hard on yourself, Laura.

I mean, I realize it was a pretty big mistake and everything, but God has really used it in your life and for others too. And I happen to think you're a much better person now than you were before."

She laughed. "Well, I kind of agree with you there."

"So, hang in there, okay?"

"Thanks, Chloe."

"And I'll keep praying for Christine."

"Yeah. Me too."

And now I'm reminded of how much we need to encourage each other on a regular basis. I sort of forget that Laura is still going through a lot. And I had no idea that she still beats herself up over that stuff. I've decided to make a more conscious effort to encourage both Laura and Allie—as well as anyone else who seems to need it. Yes, even Tiffany Knight. And I'm sure she needs it more than anyone!

LIFTING UP
why put others down?
why add to their sadness
when we can lift them up
share with them some gladness?
why suppress a kind word?
why not lend a hand
plant some seeds of hope

and show we understand?
it only takes a moment
to give someone a smile
that they can carry with them
to help them all the while
why not lift a burden
take the load off others?
love makes all the difference
to our sisters and our brothers

cm

Sunday, February 13

(PLANS OF MICE AND GIRLS)

Josh came home unexpectedly this past weekend. My parents had planned a Valentine's weekend getaway for the two of them, and although I had assured everyone that I'd be just fine on my own for a couple of days, Josh didn't want me to be home alone. That was sweet of him. His unexpected reward for coming home was that Caitlin had also come home for the weekend. A coincidence? I think not.

Neither of them had any idea that the other one was coming, and then Josh and I went to the Paradiso for breakfast on Saturday and ran into Caitlin and Beanie. A God-thing? Most definitely. I get such a kick out of watching Josh and Caitlin together. It's so obvious that they love each

other. And yet they are so mature and controlled
about it. Sometimes I just want to shove the two of
them together and say, "Why don't you just get
this over with and get married already?"
Naturally, I controlled myself.

Although I did manage to snag Beanie to talk
about our concert wardrobes. Then she and I
called up Allie and Laura and went shopping.
Beanie is so creative and free spirited! And by the
end of the day, we'd not only had a blast, but we
managed to gather up some pretty cool threads
for the next road trip.

Okay, we're still not 100 percent sure that
Laura's mom is on board, but we're praying hard
and thinking positively. And Christine's gone to
several meetings with Laura and is actually
considering a residential treatment program.
Laura even offered to pay for it out of her contract money.

This gave me an idea for Caleb, and I asked
Josh what he thought.

"That's really generous of you, Chloe," he said
yesterday. "And I don't see any problem with
bringing this up to Caleb, but I don't want you to
get your hopes up."

I nodded. "Yeah, I know. Caleb has to want
treatment or it won't work. But do you think we
could call him and ask?"

So last night, Josh called Caleb and told him

about my offer. I'd decided that I'd rather have it come from Josh than me. I listened to Josh's end of the conversation, but I could tell by his tone that it wasn't going over too well.

"Hey, we just want you to know that we love you, Caleb," he finally said. "No matter what, we love you, bro."

I was motioning for the phone now.

"Chloe wants to say something." Josh handed the phone to me.

"That's right, Caleb. I really do love you and care about you a lot. More than anything I'd like to see you get healthy."

"I appreciate that, Chloe. But I'm doing okay. I've just gotten a new job, and I'm feeling like things might be changing for me."

"Really?" I felt hopeful. "What are you doing?"

He cleared his throat. "Oh, nothing much. But it's a start, you know?"

"Would you think about my offer, Caleb?"

"Sure. I'll think about it." But I could tell by his tone that he wouldn't.

"And if you change your mind, would you call Josh? He can take care of everything, you know."

"Yeah, I know. My younger brother and sister want to take care of me." He laughed. "Guess that shows what a loser I am."

"You're not a loser, Caleb." I spoke in a firm voice now. "You are one of the coolest guys I know. I think you could do anything you put your mind to... I mean, if drugs weren't in the picture."

"You're a smart little girl, Chloe, but you don't know everything yet."

"I'm not saying I do. But I do know that drugs kill."

"Man, now you're starting to sound like a public service commercial."

"Sorry, Caleb, but it's true. Drugs kill. Maybe it just takes a little time for some people, but they kill your soul. Then they kill your mind. And eventually they may kill your body and ultimately your spirit."

"Well, thanks for the sermon, little sister. I gotta go now."

"I do love you, Caleb."

"Yeah, I love you too. But we're just different, you know? Really, really different." Then he hung up and I began to cry.

"Oh, I totally blew it, Josh. I'm sure Caleb must think I'm horrible now!" I sputtered. "I probably sounded just like Dad."

Josh came over and hugged me. "You said it just right, Chloe. Every word you said was true. And you said them in love. You couldn't have done any better."

I wiped my nose on a paper napkin and looked at Josh. "You really think so?"

"Yeah. I think God was speaking right through you. It reminded me of some of your songs. And who knows? Caleb may remember what you said and take those words to heart. All we can do is pray for him now."

And so, standing in our brightly lit kitchen, Josh and I bowed our heads and prayed for our brother. Prayed that God would break through his drugs and deception and denial and just knock that silly boy to his knees.

GET THROUGH TO HIM
do what it takes
to make him see
how much he needs You
to set him free
knock him flat
and lay him low
until he looks up
until You show
Your love to him
Your mercy and grace
when he looks up
and sees Your face
do what it takes
to make a start
to change his life
and win his heart
amen

Wednesday, February 23

(EVERYDAY LIFE)

It's amazing how quickly the newness of being at school wore off. At first it was so cool to be back in the old routines and seeing all our friends. Now after less than two months, it's starting to feel like plain old drudgery again. I'm trying to keep things in perspective—like remembering God has us here for a reason. And I do share what God's doing in my life with everyone. Even Tiffany Knight seems to be paying attention.

Just this week she asked if she could visit our church's youth group. And when I told her when and where it was, she didn't even ask me to pick her up. Not that I wouldn't. But it was a relief not to be asked. I do bring a lot of kids who can't drive to youth group. And I'm cool with that, but I'd just like to see Tiffany come to something like this on her own. Maybe just to show that she's really into it for herself and not so she can glom on to me. So there are some cool things happening here at Harrison High. But still...

I have to admit that there's a red-hot fire burning in me to get back to the concert tour. I really believe that is what God has made me for, to communicate His message through music, and I can't wait to get going again. I even miss the confines of the old tour bus, the long hours on the road, and passing through strange towns. I'm not even dreading signing autographs so much now. It's a small price to pay for performing.

Thankfully, Laura's mom seems pretty much on board now. Hopefully, Laura's had a chance to prove that she's the mature and responsible daughter her parents always believed her to be. And she is. Although you can never be totally sure about Mrs. Mitchell, since she seems to change from day to day. Just the same, I still believe that of the three of us in Redemption, Laura is by far the most mature and grounded. Well, other than that glitch with the pills—which we all believe won't happen again. And so, in some ways, life has become fairly normal and predictable.

And I'm not complaining about everyday things. I realize that's what life is made of, but there are times when God puts desires in our hearts for more. And I believe He wants us to follow those dreams.

EVERYDAY DREAMS
everyday lives doing everyday stuff
wake up, get up, sometimes it's tough
just walking and talking and hanging around
living and breathing with feet on the ground
not that i don't love these everyday things
but something inside me bursts and sings
something inside me longs for much more
to chase and discover what God has in store
everyday people with everyday eyes

can look to the heavens and reach for the skies
everyday people with so much to give
so much to love and so much to live
cm

Thursday, March 3

(I AM SEVENTEEN!)

Woowee—It's my birthday and what a groovy day
it's been! Okay, first I must admit to feeling a
little bummed for most of the day. It seemed that
no one on the planet remembered it was my birthday. My parents didn't say a word as they did their
morning routine of coffee and juice and toast.
And then I got to school and no one mentioned a
thing. Now it's not as though I'd gone around
reminding everyone that it was my birthday this
week, or even hoping they'd do something really
great. But I guess I thought someone (like maybe
Allie or Laura) might at least give me a card or a
hug or something.

I think I finally gave up all these illusions
by lunchtime. I went through the cafeteria line
by myself and got a soggy veggie burrito and
soda, then sat with Cesar and Marissa. By then
I'd accepted the gloomy fact that no one remembered what day it was and simply told myself it
was "no biggie," just get over it.

Fortunately, the day passed relatively quickly,

and I went home to get ready for band practice. Willy's been having us rehearse in the church lately since it has more room and better acoustics. But as I stopped by the kitchen for a snack, I noticed a message flashing on our answering machine. Hoping it might be some kind of birthday greeting, I played it back as I snarfed down a banana.

To my surprise it was from Eric Green at Omega announcing that Redemption had made it onto the Christian music bestsellers list for our CD!!! Okay, we were only number eighteen on the list, but still it was something. And apparently Omega was pretty impressed since we've only been out for about six months. And as a result, they have already scheduled our next recording session for this month.

"We want you girls to come out to Nashville a couple weeks before the next leg of your tour is scheduled to begin," said Eric's smooth southern voice. "That way you can cut your next CD. And by the way, Chloe, Willy suggested I leave this message with you because it's your birthday today. So happy birthday, girl! Looks like you kids are going to be climbing the charts before long. Congratulations!"

Well, I was just a whooping and a hollering (Nashville style) as I grabbed up my guitar and stuff to head for practice. I couldn't wait to see the others and start celebrating.

But when I got to the church, no one was there. Now, I sorta started feeling as though I'd stepped into the Twilight Zone since I knew it was the right place, right time, and everything. I went around to the church office to find Ginger, the church secretary.

"Oh, Chloe," she said. "Willy had to cancel the practice, and Allie called and left a message for you to meet her at the Paradiso. I guess she needs a ride."

So I hurried on over to the Paradiso, thinking at least I'd get to share the good news with someone. But when I got there the place was packed out, and I actually had to park a couple blocks away. Pretty odd for a weekday.

Then as soon as I walked in the door, everyone shouted, "Happy birthday!" As it turned out, almost everyone I knew was there, including my parents, and even Josh had made a special trip down. It was totally cool. So I had not only the greatest birthday party ever, but a real celebration over our music as well. What a day!

Monday, March 7

(HANGING IN THE BALANCE)

I know I should be flying high right now, but there's a fly in the ointment (as my Grandma

Brown would say). Hopefully, it'll fly away before it's too late for Redemption. But for the time being, meaning today, Mrs. Mitchell is still not "100 percent sure" that Laura should continue in the band. Lately she's been fretting over Laura's "slightly deteriorated grades and the disruption of her upcoming graduation plans."

"I just feel that all this music nonsense is ruining Laura's senior year," Mrs. Mitchell said yesterday as Laura and I hung out in their kitchen, attempting to persuade this woman to understand our perspective.

Of course, I wanted to tell Laura's mother that our music is NOT nonsense, and that God has given us a gift that we are trying to use wisely. But instead, I let Laura plead her case, which she did and rather eloquently too. Still, her mother was not convinced.

"Have you prayed about it, Mrs. Mitchell?" I finally asked.

"Of course," she assured me. "I am seeking God's will for my daughter's future."

I just nodded, but I wanted to say, "What about your daughter seeking God's will for her own life?"

I mean, how is it that parents can actually seek God's will for their nearly grown children's lives? Isn't that something that every individual must discover for herself? Oh, I know that we need counsel and guidance. But it seems to me that we must ultimately learn to uncover God's will individually. And I think that's what we've been trying to do—all of us—Allie, Laura, and me. Sure, we've made some mistakes along the way. Who hasn't? But I do think we're on track now. And more than ever, I believe God is leading us into something bigger than we can begin to imagine.

Before I left, I almost said to Mrs. Mitchell, "Maybe there are things more important than planning what dress you're going to wear to your graduation." It's probably wise that I didn't. And, okay, maybe I'd feel differently if it were my own graduation, but I doubt it. It seems to me that Laura's mom is getting caught up in the little things and not even seeing the bigger picture here. I could tell that Laura was close to tears when I left. She thinks this is all her fault.

"Don't worry," I told her. "Remember what God's Word says about it. Let's just keep praying."

And in an attempt to heed my own advice (actually God's), I prayed as I drove home. I prayed that God's will happens in our lives. And now I'll simply have to trust Him to do it.

TRUSTING PLACE
a place of trust
i choose to live
where it's a must

to forgive
a place of trust
i will remain
despite my fear
despite my pain
a place of trust
where i can rest
rely on Him
who knows me best
a place of trust
the only place
where i can see
my Father's face
cm

The publisher and author would love to hear your
comments about this book. *Please contact us at:*
www.letstalkfiction.com

Discussion Questions

1. Chloe is uncomfortable signing autographs for fans. Why do you think she feels this way? How would it make you feel if you were in her shoes?

2. Laura has a hard time adjusting to the concert tour. Was there something she might have done early on to avoid some of her later problems?

3. While on the road, Chloe begins to feel compassion for the homeless. What do you do if someone sp'anges you? How do you feel about street people?

4. Chloe has mixed feelings for Cesar. Do you think she was right to break things off with him? Why or why not?

5. How did you feel when you discovered that Laura was sneaking Allie's Ritalin? Did this make you think less of her? Feel sorry for her? What?

6. Chloe suspects Laura is taking Allie's pills, but Laura denies it when Chloe confronts her. What should Chloe have done at that point? What would you do if you thought a close friend had a drug problem?

7. Somehow Chloe always manages to keep her creativity flowing. How do you think she does this? What makes you feel creative?

8. Chloe begins to experience a crush on Jeremy Baxter. Do you think she should let him know how she feels? Why or why not?

9. Do you think the band handles it right when Laura confesses her drug problem? Should she have experienced more consequences?

10. With all the ups and downs that Chloe experiences, what keeps her from falling apart? What keeps you centered when everything's breaking loose in your life?

THE DIARY OF A TEENAGE GIRL SERIES

ENTER CAITLIN'S WORLD

DIARY OF A TEENAGE GIRL, Caitlin book one

Follow sixteen-year-old Caitlin O'Conner as she makes her way through life—surviving a challenging home life, school pressures, an identity crisis, and the uncertainties of "true love." You'll cry with Caitlin as she experiences heartache, and cheer for her as she encounters a new reality in her life: God. See how rejection by one group can—incredibly—sometimes lead you to discover who you really are.

ISBN 1-57673-735-7

IT'S MY LIFE, Caitlin book two

Caitlin faces new trials as she strives to maintain the recent commitments she's made to God. Torn between new spiritual directions and loyalty to Beanie, her pregnant best friend, Caitlin searches out her personal values on friendship, dating, life goals, and family.

ISBN 1-59052-053-X

WHO I AM, Caitlin book three

As a high school senior, Caitlin's relationship with Josh takes on a serious tone via e-mail—threatening her commitment to "kiss dating goodbye." When Beanie begins dating an African-American, Caitlin's concern over dating seems to be misread as racism. One thing is obvious: God is at work through this dynamic girl in very real but puzzling ways, and a soul-stretching time of racial reconciliation at school and within her church helps her discover God's will as never before.

ISBN 1-59052-890-6

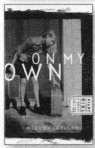

ON MY OWN, Caitlin book four

An avalanche of emotion hits Caitlin as she lands at college and begins to realize she's not in high school anymore. Buried in course-work and far from her best friend, Beanie, Caitlin must cope with her new roommate's bad attitude, manic music, and sleazy social life. Should she have chosen a Bible college like Josh? Maybe...but how to survive the year ahead is the big question right now!

ISBN 1-59052-017-3

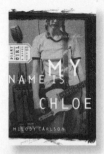

Wednesday, April 20

Is it possible that I have deceived myself into believing that God would change my personality in order to make me more acceptable to Him? Okay, I realize this sounds a bit crazy, but hang with me a minute. Because I'm thinking, okay, God did give me my personality, weird as it might be. At least I assume He did since He "knit me together in my mother's womb," and I figure that means He created my DNA, which makes me who I am. Right?

So why then would He want to change my personality? At least this is what I've been asking myself lately. People used to call me a wild child, a rebel, a nonconformist. But in some ways, I think that I've been trying to conform myself. Now what I'm wondering is, was this God's plan or mine?

The reason I'm so concerned about this is because I think it's affecting my music. And this scares me. The last thing I want is to end up sounding like everyone else, to lose my creative edge. I guess this is something I admire about Jeremy Baxter of Iron Cross. He doesn't seem to be affected in this way. It's like he doesn't compromise who he is. He remains his own self. Oh, I didn't mean to start going on about Jeremy again.

In fact, I've been doing a pretty good job of blocking my thoughts about him. Or at least I thought so. But speaking of Jeremy, I now have a new problem. I suppose it's not fair to call Isaiah Baxter a problem. Sheesh, I know that there are millions of girls who would love to have such a problem. But it seems that Allie and Laura are playing matchmaker for me. Oh, not matchmaker exactly. Rather, they are still trying to set Isaiah and me up to go to the prom.

"He said he wants to go with you," Laura said last night when we stopped for a fast-food dinner after pleading with Elise. (She thinks fast food will kill you, and she's probably not far from the truth.)

"But only if you ask him yourself," added Allie. "He doesn't want a middleman."

Fortunately, Allie, Laura, and I were seated at our own table because I'm not sure I'd want the "grown-ups" (Willy, Rosy, Elise) listening in on our conversation. I'm not even sure why.

"I don't even want to go to the prom," I told them for like the umpteenth time. "I'm not exactly a prom sort of girl, if you remember right."

"Oh, come on, Chloe," said Allie. "It's not like you have to put on a pink Cinderella dress and wear pumps."

"You have a problem with pink?" demanded Laura.

"Oh, yeah," I said. "Didn't your mom have a pink dress all picked out for you to wear to the prom?"

Laura scowled at me. "It's not so bad."

"I know." I attempted a smile on her behalf. "But the thing is I do NOT want to go to the Harrison High prom."

"Not even with Isaiah?" asked Allie.

"Yeah," said Laura. "Now, you're going to hurt his feelings."

"Hey, it's got nothing to do with Isaiah—"

"Try telling him that," said Allie.

I knew they were quickly getting me cornered. Between that proverbial rock and a hard place. "You guys are impossible!"

And so now I'm stuck here trying to decide what to do. Do I just go with the flow and invite Isaiah to the prom? I know it really doesn't mean anything from a romantic standpoint. I'm sure he knows that too. Still, it feels like it must mean something. Shouldn't you go to the prom with someone you really care about? Like Jeremy? Or even Cesar? It wasn't that long ago that I would've imagined myself going to the prom with Cesar. But true to his word, the guy is still kissing dating good-bye. Well, good for him. Maybe I should do the same.

But that brings me back to my earlier question. Like who am I? I'm afraid that I've been conforming myself into what and who other people think I should be. And the only one who should be conforming me is God. Or rather transforming me. But what if I keep getting in the way?

YOUR PLAN
change me
rearrange me
but according to Your plan
make me
just don't fake me
into something i can't stand
mold me
even scold me
if it makes me more like You
fill me
Jesus, heal me
make me real and true
amen

HEY, GOD, WHAT DO YOU WANT FROM ME?

More and more teens find themselves growing up in a world lacking in godly wisdom and direction. In *Piercing Proverbs,* bestselling youth fiction author Melody Carlson offers solid messages of the Bible in a version that can compete with TV, movies, and the Internet for the attention of this vital group in God's kingdom. Choosing life-impacting portions of teen-applicable Proverbs, Carlson paraphrases them into understandable, teen-friendly language and presents them as guidelines for clearly identified areas of life (such as friendship, family, money, and mistakes). Teens will easily read and digest these high-impact passages of the Bible delivered in their own words.

ISBN 1-57673-895-7

www.letstalkfiction.com

Let's Talk Fiction is a free, four-color mini-magazine created to give readers a "behind the scenes" look at Multnomah Publishers' favorite fiction authors. *Let's Talk Fiction* allows our authors to share a bit about themselves, giving readers an inside peek into their latest releases. To receive your free copy of *Let's Talk Fiction*, get on-line at **www.letstalkfiction.com**. We'd love to hear from you!

Tired of the game?
Kiss dating goodbye.

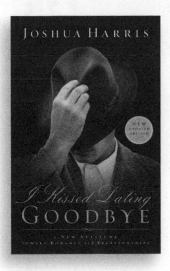

I KISSED DATING GOODBYE

Dating. Isn't there a better way? Reorder your romantic life in the light of God's Word and find more fulfillment than the dating game could ever give—a life of purposeful singleness.

ISBN 1-59052-135-8

I KISSED DATING GOODBYE STUDY GUIDE

The I Kissed Dating Goodbye Study Guide, based on Joshua Harris's phenomenal bestseller with over 850,000 copies sold, provides youth with a new resource for living a lifestyle of sincere love, true purity, and purposeful singleness.

ISBN 1-59052-136-6

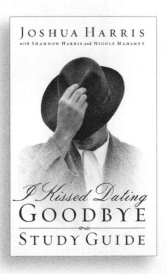

Boy meets girl. Now what?

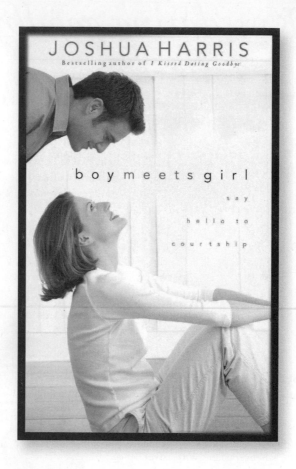

I Kissed Dating Goodbye shocked the publishing world in 1995 with its metoric rise to the top of bestseller lists. Teens wanted more than dating "rules"—they wanted an intentional, God-pleasing game plan. In this dynamic sequel, newlyweds Joshua and Shannon Harris deliver an inspiring and practical illustration of how this healthy, joyous alternative to recreational dating—biblical courtship—worked for them. *Boy Meets Girl* helps readers understand how to go about pursuing the possibility of marriage with someone they may be serious about. It's the natural follow-up to the author's blockbuster book on teen dating!

ISBN 1-57673-709-8

TRUE STORIES OF TEENS LIVING COMMITTED LIVES FOR CHRIST

stories for the extreme teen's heart

Angel Award Winner!

Celebrating Teens Who Are Saying Yes to God

Compiled by Alice Gray

Compiled with the help of teenagers, these inspiring stories show teens like you making a difference in their families, schools, and world. These compelling accounts will encourage you to a deeper walk with God, while often putting a smile on your face.

ISBN 1-57673-703-9